CONFRONTING SASQUATCH

CONFRONTING SASQUATCH

Short Fiction about Bigfoot, the Deep Woods,
and the People Who Encounter a Legend

LISA A. SHIEL

illustrations by Kerrie Shiel

Jacobsville Books

Lake Linden, Michigan
Toll-Free: 1-866-341-3705

ISBN: 978-1-934631-65-2 (pbk.)
ISBN: 978-1-934631-66-9 (e-book: EPUB)
LCCN: 2012921264

Manufactured in the United States.

Jacobsville Books
www.JacobsvilleBooks.com
1-866-341-3705

Publisher's Cataloging-in-Publication Data

Shiel, Lisa A.
    Confronting Sasquatch : short fiction about Bigfoot, the deep woods, and
the people who encounter a legend / Lisa A. Shiel ; illustrations by Kerrie
Shiel.
        p. cm.
    ISBN: 978-1-934631-65-2 (pbk.)
    ISBN: 978-1-934631-66-9 (e-book: EPUB)
    1. Sasquatch—Fiction. 2. Belief and doubt—Fiction. 3. Michigan—Fiction.
I. Shiel, Kerrie, ill. II. Title.
PS3619.H53 C66 2012
813—dc23

                                                        2012921264

Contents

Author's Note

THE STORIES IN THIS COLLECTION ARE EACH SELF-
contained entities, which means you may read them in whatever
order you like. The first six stories stand as completely separate tales,
each a world all its own. The final six stories, however, do share a
common thread—they all revolve aorund three characters from
my Human Origins Series novels. The three stories that end the book
may be read in any order, but they are best enjoyed in the order
presented, since the events in this trio of tales build on each other.

You don't need to have read my Human Origins Series novels
to appreciate the six stories that conclude this collection. They're
designed to stand on their own, as mini-introductions to the
characters and events that drive my novels.

The common thread that weaves together all twelve stories is
simulatneously simple and complex. It's the psychological impact
of a Bigfoot encounter on the person who experiences it. Belief
and doubt. Fear and curiosity. These very human traits run through
each story in this book, as the characters struggle with the tug-of-
war inside their minds.

How will each battle end? Read on to find out!

A Sense
of Direction

S HE WAS LOST. EVERY TREE LOOKED THE SAME—A PINE
was a pine, a birch was a birch. The mossy ground cover gave no
clues. The sun, masked behind thick clouds, offered no help either. In
short, April was completely, profoundly lost in the woods.

It had sounded like a good idea at the time. Pull into the state
park for a rest, go for a little hike to stretch her legs, and then head
out again. She still had a couple hours left to drive before she reached
her brother's house, and she was getting awfully tired. A little hike
would get the blood pumping. Wake her up. So she pulled into the
park, rolling her car into a slot near the restrooms. The first part of
her plan went, well, according to plan. It was the hike part that went
kablooey.

The main hiking trails all looked busy. Couples with whiny
children, college kids who made rude noises and then guffawed
at their own antics, solo men and women grimly intent on getting
exercise. All these types of people crammed onto the nice, prepared
trails. April was in no mood for company. She wanted solitude. So
she wandered off onto a trail made by deer or maybe a handful of
more adventurous hikers. It looked less popular, and therefore
quieter. Just what she needed.

The path was narrow and overgrown. She swore she saw footprints on the path, human footprints, left by someone with large, bare feet. The tracks were indistinct, though, and she might've been mistaken. That thought failed to occur to her until after she was lost. When the trail had petered out, she took a look around and decided she could find her way back anytime. She need only keep going in a straight line, then turn around and march back in the opposite direction.

Brilliant idea.

With no sun, no compass, and no GPS to guide her, she got lost faster than an envelope of cash dropped into a mailbox.

Everything looked the same.

She was no woodland newbie. She walked in the woods around her home every day, and when she visited her brother, she explored the woods around his place too. Never had she gotten lost. Never.

Clearly, not never. Not anymore.

The day felt unusually warm for March, even without the sun's heat. The snow had melted early this year throughout all of Michigan. Here in the Upper Peninsula, wherever exactly she was in the Upper Peninsula, everybody seemed keen to take advantage of the early spring. It might end tomorrow, after all, plunging the region back into winter.

The evergreens were green, of course, but the other trees had yet to sprout leaves. The grass turned green almost as soon as the snow melted, regardless of temperature, and the moss was always green. As she trudged into a small clearing, April felt the mossy ground cover squish under her boots like a wet sponge. Puddles dotted the clearing. The spring melt still hadn't soaked in completely.

She slogged through a particularly mushy patch, hopped over a puddle, and landed on more solid ground. Ahead, three large trees lay toppled. Each trunk looked as wide as April was tall, and while standing upright they must've towered at least eighty feet overhead. Now they lay in a haphazard pile, one nearly flat on the ground, another lodged against the first at an angle, and the third dangling with its crown stuck on a pine tree. She navigated around the obstacle.

Being lost had felt like an adventure—for the first ten minutes. By that point, she realized just how lost she'd gotten herself. The plan to turn around and head straight back in the opposite direction got a little skewed somewhere along the way. Following her own tracks proved impossible. The moss failed to hold tracks. If she could've reached the damp earth on the trail, she might've spotted some of her own footprints there. Unfortunately, to get to the track-yielding earth she first needed to backtrack through the mossy section of woods. No tracks there. No way to backtrack.

That's when her big revelation hit. She was lost. In the woods. Alone.

The cell phone.

The thought had struck her as she stood motionless amid the moss, surrounded by leafless trees that all appeared to be identical twins of each other—and of every tree she'd passed so far. Digging the phone out of her purse, which she carried slung over her neck with the strap crossing her chest on a diagonal, she punched buttons on the phone's face. The device made a noise. The words "no signal" appeared on the screen.

A string of curses popped into her mind. She swallowed them all.

Periodically over the last hour, she'd checked the phone. Each time the device virtually laughed at her, mocking her with its pronouncement of "no signal."

Her legs ached. Sweat beaded on her forehead. A single drop oozed down her temple. Swiping away the perspiration, she paused to lean against a birch tree. Its bark was peeling off in strips. She could tear off a strip and, with the pen in her purse, write out her last will and testament. At least then the unlucky soul who stumbled on her body days or weeks from now would know her wishes. Not that she had much in the way of property to disburse. Of course, by the time anyone else traversed this area, her body might've been eaten by wolves or ravens or some other woodland scavenger.

She was not going to die. Sooner or later she'd come upon a road. Wouldn't she?

She sank to the ground, suddenly too weary to remain upright. Her tombstone would read, "She was dumb and got lost, but her carcass fed a lot of endangered species."

Too exhausted to shake her head in disgust at the thought, she simply closed her eyes.

Crack.

The sound came from nearby. She didn't move for a couple seconds, her brain stuck in neutral. The crack sounded like a large twig, or a small branch, being snapped in two. A wild animal might've stepped on the twig.

Or a human being might've.

She opened her eyes and leaped to her feet. Glancing around, she saw nothing.

"Hello?" she called.

Rustling. To her left.

She repeated, "Hello?"

Silence.

Her heart pounded. She stumbled a few steps closer to area from which the sounds had originated. No noises emanated from the spot now.

"Is anyone there?" she said.

"Huh-huh-grrrruh," came the response.

The vocalization was soft, guttural, barely audible. She knew she'd heard it, though. It wasn't her imagination.

Unless she was more than lost. Unless she was delusional too.

She must've lost her mind as well as her sense of direction. Why else would she wander off the marked trails, with no compass and no food, all by herself? Only nutbars and total morons did that.

Was crazy better than stupid?

The breezed carried with it the susurrations of someone breathing. Nearby. From the direction of the other sounds she heard a moment ago. Someone or something hid behind a screen of evergreens.

Several possibilities came to mind. Another lost soul, too embarrassed to reveal himself or herself. A psycho stalking the woods for prey. A wild animal stalking the woods for prey.

She remembered hearing about supposed sightings of cougars in this area. Wolves lived here too. And black bears could lash out if a person accidentally got between a mother bear and her cub, or a hungry bear and his latest kill.

April stood maybe thirty feet from the stand of fir trees that her stalker used as a screen. If the stalker was a crazed murderer, she'd already revealed her presence. If the stalker was a wild animal, it already knew she was here too, even before she'd spoken.

She took a deep breath. Then she called out, "If you're there, please come out. I just want to talk."

A grunt. Snuffling. Scraping.

The stand of evergreens shimmied as something behind them moved.

A shiver raked through April. She scuffled backward, away from the fir trees.

The sunlight filtering through the clouds darkened. The breeze suddenly felt colder. She knew it was probably her nerves making everything seem darker and colder, more forbidding. But when she glanced at the sky, she noted how they had thickened, their bottoms now a darker shade of gray.

Maybe it wasn't her nerves.

Crunch. Crunch. Squish. Crunch.

She looked at the screening fir trees. Their branches waggled with referred motion. From behind the trees, footfalls crunched and every so often squished as the feet in question trod through puddles or mushy moss.

Another shiver rattled through her. It was coming for her.

She whirled and ran.

Dodging trees, resisting the urge to glance back, she raced onward without any notion of where she was going. Her right foot caught on a tree root. She stumbled, flung out a hand to grab for anything, and felt her feet flip out from under her.

She smacked into the ground face-first.

For precious seconds, she felt paralyzed. Her mind went blank. Then she finally remembered to breathe, and oxygen flooded back into her brain.

She pushed up into a sitting position. Her cheek burned. She touched it, feeling a scrape that stretched clear across her cheek from jaw to cheekbone.

The root she'd tripped over belonged to a tree that stood an arm's length away. Using the trunk for leverage, she rose to her feet.

Pain shot through her right ankle and up her leg. She cried out, doubled over, and collapsed onto the ground again. Gingerly, she explored the ankle with her fingertips. It seemed okay, so she tried to bend her ankle.

Hot spikes of pain seared her nerves. A cry welled in her throat, but she quashed it. Grimacing, she bit her lip. Great. Not only did she get lost in the woods, but now she managed to injure herself. How in hell could she find her way out of these damn woods if she couldn't walk?

The hairs on the back of her neck stiffened. Goosebumps prickled her arms.

She was not alone.

Maybe she could walk off the pain. If not...

She still had to move. Fast.

Hugging the tree trunk, she hauled herself up and onto her feet. Pain tore through her from ankle to knee. Her leg buckled, but she clung to the trunk, refusing to collapse again. She hissed out a breath through her clenched teeth. *Walk it off,* she reminded herself. Sucking in a breath, she pushed away from the tree.

And fell flat on her face.

A curse exploded from her as pain ripped into her anew. Tears stung her eyes. She felt her stomach muscles tighten as a sob welled up inside her. Gritting her teeth, she willed the tears away. She was not going to lie here crying like an abandoned baby. In a minute or two, when the searing pain subsided and she'd gathered her wits, she would get up off the blasted ground and *move.*

A tear overflowed her eyelid, dripping onto the ground.

She squeezed her eyes shut, breathing in and out several times. As she opened her eyes, she lifted her forehead off the ground.

A shadow descended over her.

She held her breath. Behind her, something breathed.

The tears seemed to freeze in her eyes. She turned her head sideways to peer out the corner of her eye at whatever stood behind her. The tears blurred her vision, though, and all she made out was a dark silhouette taller than the average man—and much stockier. The figure had a neck so thick it seemed to blend into its shoulders.

The thing grunted.

Clenching her jaw against the pain she knew would follow, April rolled over onto her back. The pain wasn't so bad this time. Blinking away the tears, she focused on her new companion. The sight before her stunned her as deeply as the excruciating pain of her injury had.

The creature looming over her sported a full-body coat of dark brown hair. Its coat was thick like an animal's, and longer on its head. Caramel-colored eyes gazed down at her with an expression of wary curiosity. A thick brow hung low over the eyes. The nose was wider than that of any human she'd ever seen, and the lips were full and wide too. The creature looked muscular, with broad shoulders and stubby fingers. Its feet were huge, though in proportion with the rest of its body. The thing must've stood at least seven feet tall.

And it was male. *Definitely* male.

The beast bent to reach for her.

She scrambled backward, away from its grasp. Pain lanced through her ankle. Scrunching her face in agony, she forced her lungs to take in a breath. Then summoned all her strength and sprang to her feet.

Pain. White hot. Sharp as daggers.

Her vision blurred. Her ears rang. The world tilted around her. She vaguely saw the creature step toward her.

Darkness.

April opened her eyes a sliver, peeking through her lashes.

Shapes. Colors. Blurry.

She blinked slowly once, twice, three times.

The shapes coalesced into figures. People. Three of them. A man in his twenties kneeled beside her, grasping her wrist while staring at his watch, as if checking her pulse. Another man, slightly older,

squatted at her feet. He watched her with a concerned expression. A woman, perhaps in her thirties, stood behind the older man. She held a cell phone to her ear as a scowl drew lines across her forehead.

The man holding April's wrist released it. Her hand dropped to the ground. He locked his narrowed gaze on her and asked, "You okay, miss?"

"Yes, I think so." April pushed up onto her elbows. "Where am I?"

"A little ways from the trailhead. Parking lot's right over there."

The man waved past her feet, where a prepared trail led through the trees toward a brighter area that must've been the parking lot.

"Ankle's swollen," the man at her feet said.

Duh, she almost said, but then decided against it. The obviousness of her swollen ankle notwithstanding, the man was trying to be helpful.

The woman clapped her phone shut. She said, "No signal out here. You'd think the parking lot would have service."

The man kneeling beside April gazed down at her. "What's your name?"

"April Clark."

"Randy Sadler." He offered a hand to her and she shook it. He nodded at the other man and said, "This is my brother Doug, and the girl with the phone is our sister Hannah."

"Nice to meet you," April mumbled. She blinked and tried to make sense of the situation. She felt a bit like she was dreaming, though the throbbing in her ankle belied that notion. "How did I get here?"

Randy glanced at his brother. "You don't know?"

April shook her head.

Pursing his lips, Doug exchanged a glance with his brother. Randy asked her, "What's the last thing you remember?"

"I was in the woods. Lost." A memory flashed in her mind—a hairy creature reaching for her. She would hardly tell Randy and his siblings about *that*. Instead, she told him, "I tripped and hurt my ankle. The pain was so bad, I guess I passed out."

"And you have no recollection of how you got here?"

"Uh-uh."

Doug chimed in now, his tone authoritative. "Probably hit her head when she passed out. A concussion can cause short-term memory loss."

April stared at the man. "Are you a doctor?"

Randy snorted. "Don't listen to him. He's a general contractor who thinks he knows everything about everything just because he knows how to google and he gets the Discovery Channel."

The expression on Doug's face became indignant, but he said nothing.

April glanced at the men's sister. Hannah, arms folded over her chest, observed the proceedings from a few yards away. A half smile tugged at her lips.

Randy stood and offered both hands to April. She took his hands, and he helped her get to her feet. His hands held onto hers as he let a slight smile curve his lips.

"We can drive you to the hospital," Randy said.

"That's okay." She tested her ankle by settling her weight on it. Pangs webbed through her ankle, but the pain was much less than before. "I'll be fine. Just need some ice for my ankle."

"We've got some in our camper." He slipped an arm around her waist. "I'll help you get there."

"Thanks."

Doug glanced past the area where she'd been lying. His eyes narrowed. Rising to a half crouch, he crab-walked several yards past where she'd lain and halted. He touched his fingertips to the ground.

"What is it?" Randy asked.

Frowning, Doug studied the ground for several seconds. Then he hopped up and walked back toward the others.

"Nothing," Doug said. "Thought I saw tracks. But unless somebody was walking around barefoot, I think it's just some smeared animal tracks. Somebody's dog maybe."

Doug marched past them. Hannah followed Doug, leaving Randy and April to bring up the rear. The sun peeked out from behind the clouds. April glanced up at it. Great, now the sun came out.

Randy's arm tightened around her, pressing her closer against him. She needed the support, but it felt odd to have a stranger's arm around her—and even odder to feel his body pressed up against hers. She glanced up at him sideways. He was cute, she noted, not that attractiveness mattered. He seemed sweet too, which mattered a whole lot more.

Cuteness didn't hurt though.

Hannah glanced at them over her shoulder. Grinning, she met April's gaze and said, "Randy's single, you know."

Randy groaned. "Maybe April's married. Did you ever think of that, Hannah?"

"She's not wearing a ring. Are you married, April? Or otherwise spoken for?"

April felt a blush heat her cheeks. "Uh, no."

Hannah grinned again, then faced front.

Clearing his throat, Randy shifted uneasily but kept his grip on April. He murmured, "Sorry about that."

"It's okay."

As they approached the trailhead, moving step by awkward step, April gazed out into the woods. Had she dreamed the encounter with the hairy creature? Maybe Doug was right after all, and she did hit her head when she passed out.

Yet Doug thought he saw barefoot tracks. April had seen similar tracks on her way out into the woods. The creature she recalled meeting would've left large, humanoid tracks.

Someone carried her from the depths of the woods to this place, near the parking lot where a good samaritan might find her. Good samaritans, to be precise. Three of them.

"What's wrong?" Randy asked.

She shrugged. "Just wondering what happened to me. How I got back here, I mean."

"Does it matter?" He squeezed her briefly in a kind of mini-hug. "You're safe. I say forget about the rest and let me make you some dinner. How do you feel about charred hot dogs?"

She smiled up at him. "I love them."

As they shambled across the parking lot toward a dirt-speckled RV, April allowed herself one last glance into the woods. She had seen the creature. It was real. Every one of her senses, perhaps even the sixth one, told her as much. The realization led to another, more startling conclusion. Maybe one day, if she got to know Randy better, she'd tell him the story. If he was as nice as she sensed he was, he'd believe it when she told him about the day she got lost in the woods.

And a Bigfoot rescued her.

Sometimes, the ridiculous turned out to be the truth.

Ethnic Food

THE WOODS WERE GLOOMY, DIRTY, AND NOISY. IN THE movies, the forest always looked beautiful and peaceful, with wild animals frolicking alongside Nordic maidens. Rob had yet to see a single maiden, and the wild animals seemed to hate him on sight. A squirrel in a nearby pine tree certainly detested him, the way it kept scolding him with its hyper chattering. As for the tranquility...

A bark of laughter exploded behind him.

Rolling his eyes, Rob half turned to face his two friends who trailed in his wake. Jason Lozio, the one who laughed like a crazy German shepherd, bent forward and slapped his own belly. The curls of his dark hair bounced with each tremor of laughter.

Mark Chao stood beside Jason, shaking his head.

"That's the dumbest thing I've ever heard," Mark said. "There's no such thing as Australian cuisine."

"Sure there is." Jason straightened, his expression mock serious. "What about shrimps on the barbie?"

"Did Crocodile Dundee ever eat shrimp? No, and I'll tell you why. Because it's sissy food."

Jason snorted but, thankfully, didn't laugh again.

Rob adjusted the straps of his backpack, which had started to dig into the soft flesh of his underarms. Maybe the ten tons of crap crammed into his backpack had something to do with it. Did anyone really need five boxes of granola bars and four one-pound Hershey bars? Then there was the ridiculous equipment, stuffed into each of their backpacks with flannel shirts and hoodies for padding. Rob's pack held binoculars, a thing that looked like a video camera but that Jason swore was a night vision something-or-other, and various other devices about which even Jason seemed to have no clue.

Granted, the binoculars seemed like a reasonable choice. But the rest looked like it came straight out of a catalog for redneck James Bond wannabes. And naturally, Jason forgot to buy the one piece of equipment that might have actually helped them—a GPS unit.

Rob knew they were somewhere inside Porcupine Mountains Wilderness State Park in the Upper Peninsula of Michigan. But after walking all morning, who knew where they ended up. They might've been walking in circles, or they might've hiked into Wisconsin by now.

"You have to pick something else," Mark said. "Australian food can't be your favorite because it doesn't exist."

Jason shrugged. "Okay, then it's Chinese."

Mark groaned.

"Come on." Jason bumped his fist into Mark's shoulder. "How can you not like Chinese, man? It's your heritage."

"My family emigrated long before your grandfather stopped selling pizzas to Mussolini."

"He didn't sell pizzas to anybody, he was an accountant. Besides, my mom's side of the family got here in 1773."

Mark scrunched his face and feigned agony. "Please spare us from hearing the 2,056th retelling of how your ancestor Ebenezer what's-his-face saved Massachusetts from the Red Coats."

Snap!

Rob jerked. The sound came from further into the woods, where shadows and branches concealed everything from view. He glanced around the woods, squinting as he tried to sort out the visual mishmash. The snap had sounded like a large twig or a small branch breaking. Yet he saw nothing. It didn't seem windy enough to snap a branch. Maybe a deer stepped on a twig.

Returning his attention to his friends, Rob wondered for the umpteenth time today just what the hell they were all doing out here. Off and on for the past three hours, he had been listening to Jason and Mark bicker over what type of ethnic food they preferred. He glanced at his watch. No, make that three and half hours. Strangers listening in on the conversations might think the men hated each other. But the three of them have been friends since high school. They even worked at the same tech company.

Mark rubbed his tummy. "I could go for some Italian right about now."

"Great," Jason said. "Maybe you can beg some pizza off of Mussolini."

"Mussolini's dead, you moron."

Rob cleared his throat loudly. "Remind me again what the purpose of this trip was."

Jason grinned. "We're getting out of the city to commune with nature, bro."

Although Rob despised being called bro, he bit back the retort that rose in his throat. He did not want to get distracted by another one of Jason's long-winded discourses. He wanted the details Jason had thus far kept to himself about the purpose of their trip.

"We could've done that back in Oklahoma," Rob said. "Why'd we have to fly to Michigan for it?"

"Yeah," Mark chimed in, "and what's all the equipment for?"

Jason grinned some more, bobbing on his toes.

"Spit it out," Rob said. "Or I'm leaving."

He wasn't sure he could find his way back to the parking lot, but the ultimatum sounded good.

As the grin settled into a smirk, Jason motioned for his friends to come closer. Mark edged nearer Jason, but Rob held his ground. Leaning forward a little, Jason glanced around as if checking for eavesdroppers.

Then he whispered, "Were searchin' for Sasquatch."

Rob wanted to deck him right then and there. Instead, he said, "That's what you meant when you said we were in for an epic adventure?"

"It is epic, bro. I bought all kinds of equipment to help us find and document the existence of the legendary Sasquatch. We'll be rich and famous."

Mark frowned at Jason. "There's supposed to be Bigfoot in Oklahoma, I saw it on TV. We didn't have to fly up here for that. We could've stayed home to make complete fools of ourselves, minus the air sickness and the high cost of travel."

Jason shook his head. "You guys have no sense of adventure. I read on the Internet there were a bunch of sightings up here."

"When?" Rob asked.

"Um...I don't know, the site didn't really say."

"Are you kidding me? You dragged us up here based on some vague bull—"

Crack.

They all froze. The sound had originated to Rob's left, behind a large pine tree, less than twenty feet away from them.

Rob whispered, "What was that?"

For a couple seconds, Jason stared wide-eyed at the pine tree. Then he shrugged, making a dismissive noise. His face had gone pale, however, and even his lips appeared less pink than usual.

Jason coughed and said, "Probably just a grizzly."

"They don't have grizzly bears in Michigan," Mark said. "Just black bears and wolves."

Rob felt his stomach lurch upward. "Terrific, getting eaten by wolves sounds a lot more macho than getting eaten by a grizzly."

Mark patted Rob's arm. "Don't worry, wolves are just overgrown puppies. Cute and fuzzy, you know."

"I'll remind you of that when the wolves are dining on your spleen."

Jason chuckled, though it sounded more nervous than sarcastic. "Ethnic food. The wolves can have some Chinese spleen, a little Italian intestine, and some haggis."

"Haggis?" Mark said.

Jason nodded in Rob's direction. "Mister McKendrick over there is Scottish."

Behind the pine tree, something moved.

Mark started to speak, but Rob raised a hand to silence them. He thought he saw a dark shape behind the tree, a partial outline of...something.

His voice barely audible, Jason asked, "What?"

"Something there," Rob said, pointing behind the tree.

His friends stared at the spot he pointed to, but the shape had disappeared.

Jason grabbed a stout stick from the ground and marched around the pine tree before Rob could say anything. Mark gasped.

The only sounds Rob could hear were Jason's footfalls and the pounding of his own heart.

Brandishing a stick like a baseball bat, Jason stepped out of sight behind the tree.

"Ahhh!"

Jason's cry pierced the air. Rob couldn't move. Couldn't think. He should do something, but what?

A second ticked by. Then two.

Laughter erupted behind the tree.

Jason staggered out into the open, clutching his gut, tears streaming from his eyes. For a moment, Rob thought his friend was injured. Finally, Jason raised a hand to point to his friends.

Between gasps of laughter, Jason said, "You should see the looks on your faces. Rob thought a Sasquatch got me, didn't you?"

"I wish." Rob peered into the foliage behind Jason. "I did see something, though."

"It was a raccoon."

Jason walked toward his friends. Then he halted, he dropped his backpack onto the ground and unzipped the main compartment. After several minutes of digging around inside the pack, he extracted a device that looked sort of like a price gun stores used to stick price tags on merchandise, back when they used to have price tags.

"What's that?" Rob asked.

"Thermal imaging camera. It'll let us see what's out there, even if it's hiding."

Jason stood up, and turned on the device. The little screen showed a black-and-white image of the woods. Jason swung the camera toward Mark, and he showed up as a white silhouette in the black-and-white image.

Closing up his backpack, Jason slung it over one shoulder. "Let's get moving again. We won't find Sasquatch unless we go looking for him."

"Do you even know what you're doing?"

"Sure, I read about it online."

Rob groaned. Wonderful. Rob got his Sasquatch-hunting skills from a website.

"It's okay," Jason said. "We're professionals."

"We are professional computer programmers. Not—not—whatever you need to be to hunt for Sasquatch."

"It's a calling, not a career."

Jason led them past the pine tree and down a narrow trail through the woods. Rob supposed deer had made the trail, since it was barely wide enough for a person. As they walked, Jason swung his thermal imaging camera left and right. Every so often, Rob caught a glimpse of the camera's screen. No white spots. They seemed to have scared off all the wildlife, even the grumpy squirrel.

"So," Mark said, "it's Italian then. I saw a restaurant along the highway."

His gaze still locked on the thermal imaging camera, Jason replied, "No, no, we are not eating Italian. How about Cornish? I saw a deli that was selling pasties."

"Yuck. I'd rather eat duct tape."

"That can be arranged," Rob said. "I think Jason stuffed some in my backpack."

Jason stopped so abruptly that Mark bumped into his back. Rob managed to skid sideways to avoid the other two.

Mark peered over Jason's shoulder at the thermal imaging camera. His mouth dropped open.

Scuffling forward, Rob sidled up to Jason. He looked down at the screen on the camera.

In the center of the screen hulked a pale silhouette.

Rob gazed past the camera at the area displayed on its screen. A forest of saplings, none thicker than Rob's thumb but all sporting a mesh of leaves, blocked the view.

On the camera's screen, the silhouette appeared to stand behind the saplings, directly ahead of them.

Jason panned the camera left. Another silhouette appeared. Then another. He panned it right, past the silhouette that stood directly in front of them. Another pair of white shapes popped out behind the trees there.

A shiver rattled down Rob's spine.

"Let's get out of here," Mark said.

Jason nodded. "I second that."

Still holding the camera in front of him, Jason spun around and marched past his friends. Just as they began to hurry after him, Jason slid to a halt. On the camera's screen, white shapes loomed up ahead.

Scuffling sounds emanated from the woods around them.

Rob's heart pounded. The blood thundered in his ears. Holy heaven, what had they gotten themselves into? Looking for Bigfoot in the woods, when none of them had set foot in any kind of woods for years. They sat in cubicles eight hours a day, without even a window to let them glimpse the outdoors.

Something growled.

Mark let out a ragged whimper.

Rob followed Mark's gaze rightward. In full view in front of a tree, no more than a dozen feet away, stood a Sasquatch.

Jason whispered, "What does it want?"

`A tone of panic infused his voice. Rob glanced at his friends. Their faces were as pale as he felt sure this must be. His hands trembled. He forced himself to look back at the creature staring them down from a dozen feet away.

What *did* it want?

The creature's nostrils flared as it sniffed the air. The beast fixed its gaze on Rob.

A chill raced through him.

Mark whimpered again. "I think it wants *you*, Rob."

"For what?" he asked, though he felt certain he did not under any circumstances want to know the answer.

Jason let out a nervous chuckle. His voice quavered as he said, "Ethnic food."

The creature tilted its head, narrowing its eyes.

Mark stumbled backward. "Screw this."

He bolted through the woods.

Jason took off after him. Rob kept pace with Jason, his legs pumping so hard they ached, his breath coming shallow and fast. He felt an urge to look back, but he quashed it. No way would he look back. No way in hell.

He swore he heard footfalls whumping behind him.

Do not look back.

Something yanked on his backpack. His feet flipped out from under him. Whatever had grabbed his pack now flipped him over onto his stomach. He felt a hairy hand graze his neck and cheek. The fingers closed around his backpack strap, where it met the pack. The hand jerked. The strap snapped free.

The creature grasped the other strap and snapped it too.

He felt the weight lift as the backpack was hefted off of him.

The creature shuffled away from him. Grunting ensued, intermingled with scraping and tearing.

He heard the backpack's zipper open.

More grunting. The sound of paper ripping.

Rob cautiously turned his head sideways. Maybe ten feet away, the Sasquatch crouched with the backpack on the ground in front of him. The beast had torn several holes in the pack before he managed to unzip the main compartment. Now, in one stubby hand the creature held one of the Hershey bars. The packaging was ripped open, exposing the milk chocolate inside.

The creature broke off a hunk of chocolate. He sniffed it. With a humanlike look of interest, he licked the chocolate. Then, he shoved the whole piece into his mouth and chewed.

The creature made a sound that Rob swore was "mmm."

A scream reverberated through the woods.

Not Jason or Mark. The scream sounded inhuman, though not like any animal Rob had ever heard either.

The creature looked up. He listened for a few seconds, then tilted his head back and let out a matching scream.

Rob slapped his hands over his ears. The sound was unbelievably loud.

The Sasquatch dug the rest of the candy bars out of the backpack. He leaped up and loped off into the woods.

Rob stayed on the ground, watching until the creature disappeared from sight. He waited another minute or two just to be sure.

He pushed onto his knees. The backpack was trashed. He didn't care about that. He had to find Mark and Jason.

Footfalls crashed through the brush to his right.

He grabbed a stick, brandishing it like a sword. Which was stupid. If one of those things came back for him, a two-foot-long stick wouldn't faze it.

Mark and Jason stumbled out of the trees. Gasping, they halted a few feet from Rob.

Jason wheezed, "You okay, man?"

Rob nodded. "You?"

Both men nodded.

Jason gripped the thermal imaging camera in one hand. He panned it back and forth.

"All clear," he said. "But let's get out of here now. Before they come back."

Rob clambered to his feet. Mark and Jason headed into the woods. Abandoning his backpack, Rob hurried after them. By some miracle, they found the parking lot without too much trouble. The journey back took less than an hour, which cemented Rob's feeling that they had been walking around in circles in the woods. He didn't care anymore, though. He just wanted to go home.

They hardly said a word to each other on the hike back to the parking lot, or during the drive back to the motel, or on the drive from there to the airport, or on the flight back to Oklahoma. Even when they returned to work on Monday morning, they exchanged little more than pleasantries. Rob supposed it would take longer than thirty-six hours for the shock to wear off completely. Maybe it never would.

He had just sat down in his cubicle that morning when another co-worker stopped by to greet him. It was Heather, the college intern. She leaned over the cubicle wall, folding her arms atop it.

"Morning," she said. "I'm buying lunch for everybody today. How does Chinese sound?"

Rob swallowed against the lump that suddenly formed in his throat. "No ethnic food, if you don't mind. Burgers and fries would suit me fine."

She scrunched her eyebrows. "You sure?"

"Positive."

"Okay."

Heather skipped off down the aisle.

Rob faced his computer. From this day forward, the term ethnic food would take on a whole new meaning. He might never eat fried rice or lasagna again.

And he would certainly, without any doubt at all, never ever set foot in the woods again.

The next time Jason wanted an epic adventure, he'd book them a trip to Disney World.

Danger
Signs

T HE MORNING WAS COOL, AND SHE PULLED HER JACKET
tighter around her. Emily hopped down the three steps from
the porch to the ground. Dew beaded on the windshield of her
car, parked fifteen feet from the porch. The crescent moon hung
low in the sky, a hair above the treetops. Songbirds twittered
overlapping tunes. Emily surveyed the little clearing around her
two-story farmhouse and smiled. It was a good morning for a
walk in the woods.

Hands in her jacket pockets, she took three steps away from the
porch—and stopped.

She studied the sight that had halted her. Three sticks lay on top of
the gravel of the driveway. The sticks were equal in length and width,
about half an inch thick and six inches long, and they appeared to have
been snapped off longer branches. Two of the sticks formed a V shape,
while the third stuck straight out from the open side of the V. It looked
like a little arrow, pointing toward the woods in front of the house.
Pointing toward the deer trail she normally followed on her walks. Had
someone placed the sticks there?

Oh brother. The sticks must've blown there or been dropped there
by a bird. They just happened to land in a shape she interpreted as an

arrow. Boy, if she let her imagination get the better of her, she could really go on a paranoia field trip.

She brushed the sticks out of the driveway with the side of her shoe. They landed haphazardly in the grass.

With a sigh, she headed toward the deer trail thirty feet to the right of the driveway. The trail was narrow, and if the brush grew any higher or thicker she might have to find another path for her walks. Either that, or she'd need to buy a garden tractor so she could mow the trail. For now, she pushed the thought out of her mind. The woods beckoned her.

At the trailhead, she hesitated. There, in the grass alongside the trail, lay two sticks crossed in an X shape. Like the sticks she found in the driveway, these were six inches long and half an inch thick.

No sticks occupied that spot the day before. She knew because she walked this trail every morning and because she always glanced at this spot to admire the tuft of delicate blue wildflowers that grew here.

So the sticks hadn't been there before. So what? She must be in a weird mood this morning.

Kicking the sticks aside, she marched down the trail. It wound through the woods for a third of a mile, then dead-ended at a gravel road. At the road, she turned left to continue her walk on the shoulder. Daisies bloomed in the roadside ditch. On her way back, she might pick some.

Up ahead, a car sat parked on the edge of the road, with its left tires in the ditch.

Emily stopped. She didn't recognize the car. Most of the folks who lived on this road drove SUVs or trucks. This car looked sporty, though dated. The paint was chipped, the metal rusted in places. As she approached the car, she noticed the left rear tire was flat. The driver's door hung ajar a few inches.

Her pulse quickened. She thought about turning around, then decided she ought to check in case someone was injured. Tiptoeing to the bumper, she peered through the rear window into the car. It looked empty. She glanced into the ditch but saw nothing there either. Maybe someone had given the driver a ride, or the driver decided to walk to the nearest house for help.

A chill shimmied down her spine. She scanned the woods. The hairs at the nape of her neck bristled. She felt the eerie sensation of being watched by an unseen observer.

Get a grip. No one was watching her. Apparently, when she ate her cereal this morning she also swallowed a hefty dose of paranoia. Well, they said sugar was bad for you.

Still, she hiked back toward home.

Where the deer trail opened into the clearing, next to the wildflower patch, she saw something that made her freeze mid step.

Three sticks. In an arrow shape. Pointing at the house.

She lifted her head to gaze at the house. A shiver swept through her.

Oh come on. Somebody probably planted the sticks as a joke.

Which would mean someone was prowling around in the woods on her property. Watching her. Quietly laughing at her. Feeling superior.

Emily sprinted to the house, leaped up the steps, flung open the front door, dashed inside, and slammed the door behind her. Leaning back against the door, she reached behind her to click the lock into place. Then she squatted to untie her shoelaces.

Faint shoe prints etched a trail away from the door.

They weren't her tracks. These prints were larger, with a different tread pattern.

She whirled to face the door, scrambling for the lock. Her fingers trembled, and she couldn't get ahold of the lock release. Her heart pounded. Her fingers fumbled and slipped.

The stench of liquor and cigarettes overwhelmed her a second before the weight slammed into her. She smacked into the door face-first.

A man's voice rasped in her right ear. "I seen you. Out there."

The man spun her around, pinning her against the door with one arm. His other hand gripped a revolver.

She quickly cataloged his appearance. Dark, scraggly hair. Ratty beard. Faded T-shirt and jeans. He trembled and sweat dribbled down his face. He looked skinny, almost emaciated, and pale. His brown eyes were oddly dilated.

He pointed the gun at her face. "Gimme it. Now."

"Give you what?"

"You can't get away so just give it to me."

The muzzle of the revolver pointed at her nose. She looked at the man, the gun, the man, the gun.

Stumbling backward away from her, he waved the gun wildly in the general direction of the living room. "Get in there."

She scuffled into the living room. He gestured at the sofa and she sat down, perched on the edge of the cushions. The intruder ran to the window, crouching down to peek out, then scuttled into the center of the room.

"Where are they?" he hissed. "I know you told them. Just gimme the stuff and it'll be over. The toaster broke yesterday. "

The guy must be high on something, she decided. How stupid had she been? She suspected someone was prowling around the house, so what did she do? Run inside and lock herself in with a psycho.

She couldn't have known he was in here. Deep down, she'd assumed a teenage boy may be responsible for the arrow-shaped signs made out of sticks. A reasonable assumption, she'd thought. Until now.

Clasping her hands on her lap, Emily tried to sound calm as she asked, "What are you looking for?"

The man jerked his head toward her. He fixed his dilated eyes on her. Black pools of emptiness.

"I need it," he said. "Cash, jewelry, stuff."

She had five dollars in her purse and nothing but costume jewelry. What else he might want, she didn't know. Her thoughts spun and twirled in her mind, too fast for her to catch them.

The man jumped. His gaze was locked on the window. "What was that? Cops can't find me, they try but I'm too quick."

Emily gazed out the window but saw nothing. Telling him that seemed like a bad idea, though, so she kept her mouth shut. If she ran for the front door, maybe—

The man shouted a wordless cry of terror.

Her heart skipped a beat. She followed the intruder's gaze to the window. Nothing there.

The man stumbled backward, fell, scrambled to his feet. His eyes were wide, his mouth agape. He'd dropped his gun on the floor a dozen feet from Emily. She looked at the window, the gun, the man.

He stabbed a shaky finger in the air at her. "You. You're a witch. Called the monsters outta hell and they came to you. I know what you are."

She had to get away from him. Now.

He stood between her and the doorway. The gun lay equidistant from each of them. In her mind, she tried to calculate the risks of going for the gun versus waiting for the man to snap. No contest. She had to go for the gun.

Bam!

They both jumped. The intruder yelped, spinning toward the sound. It came from the hallway, and it sounded like a great weight slamming into the front door.

Bam!

This time she saw the door quiver.

The psycho shot a terrified glance at her. Spittle flew from his lips as he shouted, "Stop it, witch! I ain't going to hell, you can't make me, I'm too strong."

The weight rammed into the door one last time, then silence descended on the house.

The intruder sucked in a breath. He started to pant, as if he'd just run a great distance. His gaze was on the front door.

Emily looked at the gun. She half rose, body tensed, preparing to jump.

A shriek shattered the air. Emily winced. Though it came from outside, the shriek resonated through the house with earsplitting volume. The scream sounded inhuman, and unlike any animal cry she had ever heard.

The intruder had fallen silent. He looked dazed, frozen in place.

Emily launched herself at the gun. She grabbed it and sprang to her feet, leveling the weapon at the intruder.

He slowly turned his head toward her. He didn't look at her, but rather, past her at the window over her shoulder. What little color there was in his face drained away in an instant.

The man bolted for the front door, fumbled with the lock, finally flung open the door, and fled. His footsteps pounded

across the porch and down the steps as the door banged into the wall, bouncing off it.

Emily rotated her head to look at the window.

A creature stared back at her from outside. Creature was the only word to describe the thing. It wasn't human, and it wasn't a bear or other animal she would recognize. Humanoid in shape, the creature stood as tall as the top of the window, which rose eight feet off the ground. The creature had broad shoulders and a neck so thick it seemed almost nonexistent, as if the head sat directly on the shoulders. Hair covered the entire body, or at least all that she could see of the body, which was most of it. A thick brow protruded above the eyes.

The creature turned and walked toward the front of the house, out of sight.

Emily stood there for a moment, unable to think or move. Then, the intruder's revolver gripped in her right hand, she shuffled to the front door. It hung three-fourths open.

The creature crouched in the driveway, a dozen feet from the porch. When it saw her, it sprang up and darted off into the woods.

It took several minutes before she could summon the courage and the mental capacity to walk out onto the porch. Standing at the cusp of the steps, she stared at the spot where the creature had knelt. There, two sticks lay in a T shape.

Not until the next day did she realize the creature must've left the arrow signs for her. The first pointed into the woods, probably an attempt to warn her about the oncoming danger. The psycho must've come from the derelict car, for it was gone now. The second arrow had pointed to the house, warning her the intruder was inside. Unfortunately, the meaning of the signs eluded her—especially since she'd assumed the signs were a joke perpetrated by a bored teenager. The truth was far stranger than anything she could've imagined.

Bigfoot saved her from a psychopath.

She would never tell anyone, of course. No one would believe it. Sometimes she couldn't believe it herself. Sometimes she could half convince herself that it never happened.

But once in awhile, when she returned from a walk, she'd find a few sticks arranged in a T shape or an equals sign, placed near the tuft of wildflowers.

And she would wonder.

The Man in the Suit

EVERYBODY IN THE WORLD WORE SUITS EVERY SINGLE day. Folks wore happy suits to hide their misery, calm suits to mask their panic, and wisdom suits to conceal their ignorance. Everybody pretended the suits didn't exist, but nobody lived without the protection suits offered. Sometimes, a person might even wear an anonymity suit so no one else would recognize them. Folks most often donned those suits when writing letters or blogs, or when making phone calls. Some people might call them masks, not suits, but a mask covered only the face. A suit concealed everything.

The point was, everybody wore a suit.

So Evan felt no remorse over putting on his suit this morning. Unlike all those other folks, he never pretended the suit didn't exist. He recognized it, appreciated it, and reveled in it. Today's suit qualified as an anonymity suit. He wore it for artistic reasons, rather than to hide his identity. Performance art required a certain level of anonymity—at least the kind of performance art Evan created did. If the marks saw his face, they'd lose the fear. And the fear was essential.

Blood, sweat, and fear. His art needed those elements.

From his vantage point squatting in the bushes, Evan could see the main trail. It led deeper into the woods, into places more wild and remote than this spot. Yet the spot in which he sat offered him the best of everything—distance from the parking lot, sparse foot traffic, and just enough woods to dampen the sounds of the chaos he inflicted on his marks. This spot was also the farthest he could walk while carrying the tools of his art.

Distant voices wafted to him from down the trail. Coming this way, he realized.

Evan glanced across the trail to the thin pine tree he'd climbed earlier. His motion-activated camera hung strapped to the trunk right where'd placed it, high enough that the marks would fail to notice it. Capturing the massacre on film was vital. Okay, it was a digital video camera, but the medium hardly mattered. Once he uploaded the video to the Internet, his fame would blossom. Sure, some folks might call him immoral, but many more would appreciate the artistic chaos.

The voices drew nearer. He heard the melodic giggle of a young woman, maybe a teenager. Excellent. Chicks screamed way better than dudes. Apply a little pressure, a little terror, and most chicks let loose with the kind of piercing shriek that Evan otherwise could hear only in horror movies. He loved making them scream.

Blood, sweat, fear and *screams*. His art would be awesome today.

Evan grabbed the remote control that rested on the ground near his left foot. The device slipped out of his ungainly fingers. He snatched it up again, this time grasping it in both hands. He normally wasn't this clumsy. The suit did it to him. Taking the remote firmly in one hand, he found a small stick that he could use as a tool to press the buttons on the remote. He must wait until precisely the right moment to activate the boombox, which he'd hidden closer to the trail behind a tangle of wild blueberry bushes. The boombox provided the soundtrack for the massacre.

Further down the trail, figures moved as colored shadows.

Evan's pulse quickened. He started to rise, then caught himself. *Not yet.*

The marks stepped out into the open, fifty feet to his left. They paused to watch a woodpecker that had lighted on a dead tree. As the bird hammered away, the trio of humans whispered and pointed.

A smile crept across Evan's face. The trio consisted of an older couple and a twenty-something girl. The older man looked sixty-ish. Probably on Social Security and Medicare. Stealing money from younger folks so he could sit on his mangy duff. Evan would teach the old fart a lesson. Maybe the codger would pee his pants when Evan attacked, or have a heart attack. The world didn't need all those old codgers anyway. They were nothing but money-sucking miscreants who ruined the economy for everybody else.

Yeah, these marks were perfect. An old fart to torture, a young chick to squeeze for screams, and a third mark to watch it all.

The woodpecker flew away. The trio started down the trail toward Evan.

He waited. They ambled closer. Forty feet. He positioned the stick over the correct button on the remote control. Twenty feet. His muscles tensed in anticipation. Fifteen feet.

Evan punched the button.

An inhuman shriek split the pastoral tranquility. The shriek sounded like a cross between a woman's scream, a wolf's howl, and the bellowing of an injured grizzly bear. The boombox reproduced the shriek in lifelike clarity, though at a volume that gave the impression of distance—a little distance.

The marks froze. Eyes wide, the girl hugged herself. The old fart squinted, as if suspicious, while he glanced around the woods. The older woman muttered something Evan couldn't hear.

Evan rose. A stand of saplings shielded him from the trio's view. Dropping the stick and the remote, he picked up the prop he needed for stage two.

The shriek ended as the recording shifted into silence. A few seconds of relief before the massacre.

Taking the prop in one hand, he lumbered forward.

On the trail, the old fart said, "Sounded like a loon."

A loon? Was this guy for real?

The scream of a tortured animal echoed through the woods. Showtime.

Evan burst out of the trees onto the trail. He swung the prop over his head and grunted like a crazed baboon.

The girl screamed.

The old man gaped at Evan.

Oh yeah, this was high art. And so much damn fun too!

Evan slammed the prop down on the ground. The water balloon hidden inside the fake deer head split open, spewing faux blood. The girl screamed again. Evan stamped his feet like any self-respecting Sasquatch would.

The older woman pursed her lips. She reached inside a fanny pack and brought out a handgun.

Evan froze.

"You're no Bigfoot," the woman said, her voice calm yet hard.

Sweat dribbled down Evan's temples. This damn ape suit was hotter than an erupting volcano. And it itched. Blast it all, the suit itched something awful.

But the art was worth it. Didn't real artists have to suffer?

The woman aimed her gun at the ground in front of Evan. "Take off the monkey suit, kid."

Evan stared at the gun. Did real artists also have to die for their art? Well, a lot of them didn't get famous until after they died.

Screw that.

Evan raised his hands in surrender. "Okay, lady."

He fumbled with the head part of the suit. Then, after a couple minutes of sweating and silently cursing while the old bitty took aim, he finally managed to peel the suit's head off his own. He dropped the head on the ground.

The old guy marched past Evan. He rooted around in the brush, searched the weeds, and then stumbled onto the blueberry patch. With a triumphant smile and an "a-ha" cry, the codger lifted the boombox out of the bushes. He pushed buttons.

The inhuman shriek blasted from the speakers. The old fart hit the stop button. Silence.

Pow!

Evan jerked. His ears rang. The old bitty had shot at him.

No, wait. He traced the trajectory of her gun to its target. The boombox. She'd shot a big honking hole in his boombox.

Evan stared at the woman. He whined, "That thing cost a hundred and—"

The woman aimed her gun at his feet.

How many bullets did the gun have?

"I-I'm sorry," Evan said, as the ringing in his ears subsided. "It was a joke, that's all. I didn't mean anything by it."

The woman slipped her gun back inside the fanny pack. "Don't you ever pull a prank like this again. Got it, sonny?"

"Yes, ma'am."

The woman led her companions down the trail. Soon they hiked out of sight.

Birds chirped. The wind rustled leaves. Evan's heart pounded. He took slow, deep breaths until his pulse normalized.

The shattered boombox lay on the ground a dozen feet away. He shambled toward the boombox, nudged it with one foot. Leave it to a chick to ruin his art.

He got the recording of a so-called Bigfoot scream from a website. The dumbos on the site actually believed they'd recorded an ape-man's cries in the wilderness. Evan figured either the dumbos faked it or one of their buddies faked it just to make them look stupider than they already were. Maybe the hoaxer understood art.

Evan smirked. He'd like to meet the hoaxer. They could collaborate on a some truly fine art.

Groping behind his head, Evan tried to reach the zipper on the suit. Duh, of course he couldn't grab it with these rubber things on his hands. Yanking off the fake Sasquatch hands, he tossed them on the ground. He groped for the zipper again. His fingers closed around the zipper and he tugged on it. The zipper didn't budge. He tugged harder. No luck.

His fingers were sweaty. Wiping them dry on the fake fur of his suit, he grasped the zipper again and yanked hard. The little metal

tab broke off the zipper. Without it, he couldn't grasp the thing that
did the unzipping.

Evan flung the little tab onto the ground as he unreeled a string
of curses.

He'd have to walk back to the parking lot in full costume, the
same way he entered the woods. He felt like a water balloon, all wet
inside his suit.

By the time he'd gathered his backpack, the broken boombox,
and the video camera, he felt sure the suit itself was sweating too.
He jammed the boombox and camera in his backpack, along with
the hands and head from his suit, and slung the pack over one
shoulder.

His first attempt at performance art had bombed. Like a nuclear
warhead.

Evan headed down the trail.

Crack.

He stopped. The crack sounded like a twig breaking. A really,
really huge twig. The Bigfoot of twigs.

To his right, something growled.

His mouth went dry. He tilted his head to listen. The growling
had stopped. He heard folks say that wolves roamed these woods,
but he didn't quite believe them. They probably saw a German
shepherd that escaped from somebody's yard. The growling he just
heard sounded kind of like a dog—but much, much bigger.

The Bigfoot of dogs?

Or maybe...

Nah. The old bitty and her gun scared him, he'd admit that much,
and the whole incident left his nerves in a tangle. The sound probably
wasn't growling at all, but a tree creaking or...something.

"Uh-uh-uh."

The sound, like a grunt but not a grunt, issued from the
woods to his right. Evan licked his parched lips but, of course,
he had no saliva. In slow motion, he turned his head toward
the sound.

Framed by the branches of a tree, a face stared back at him.

Evan blinked. Swallowed. Blinked again.

The face was hairy, with a low brow that protruded over the eyes. Dark, glistening eyes. The flat nose wiggled, as if the creature were sniffing out Evan's scent.

The creature stepped out from behind the tree.

Evan couldn't move. Sweat dribbled down his face, stinging in his eyes.

The Bigfoot eyed him.

Evan screamed.

The creature shrieked.

Evan turned to run, tripped over the feet of his costume, and smacked face-first into the ground. His backpack slid off his shoulder. Dirt lodged in his mouth and nostrils. He scrambled to get up, fell again, pushed onto hands and knees.

Footfalls whumped behind him. A foul odor enveloped him. He fought back a wretch, collapsing onto his belly.

A shadow fell over him.

His heart hammered as fast as a woodpecker's beak. The earth felt clammy against his skin. He shivered, though not because of the clammy earth.

Silence.

The shadow held still. The stench clogged his nostrils, forcing him to breathe through his mouth. He waited for the beast to move. What felt like minutes ticked by, though it might've been seconds. The adrenaline coursing through him skewed his sense of time.

The beast leaned closer.

Oh God. The thought was half exclamation, half prayer.

Something, probably a hairy hand, tugged at Evan's suit—gently at first, then with more force. Evan squeezed his eyes shut. If he died while wearing a Bigfoot suit, that was bad enough. But to die in a Bigfoot suit, killed by a Bigfoot...

The creature flipped him over onto his back.

Evan mewled. He'd never heard a person make that sound before, yet it issued from his mouth.

The beast poked him in the chest.

Don't die in a Bigfoot suit.

Evan peeled his eyelids apart, millimeter by millimeter.

The Bigfoot was gone.

He glanced down at his chest. A red stripe marred the fake fur. *Blood.*

Evan almost screamed again, then froze. The blood didn't look right. He touched the smear, sniffed his fingertip, tasted the substance, and nearly sobbed with relief. The substance wasn't blood. It was the fake blood he made from raspberry jam and ketchup.

As he pushed up into a sitting position, he surveyed his surroundings. The backpack lay on the ground a few feet away. The fake deer head rested about twenty feet away. The creature must've checked out the fake deer head before coming after him. But why did the Bigfoot come for him?

The boombox. He called in a Bigfoot.

He hadn't meant to, naturally. Yet even without intending to, he succeeded where those dumbos from the website failed. He lured a Bigfoot to him.

Too bad he hadn't thought to get out the video camera. His art project might've worked out after all.

A whooping call echoed through the forest.

Goosebumps raised all over Evan's body. The whooping sounded close, though not breathing-down-his-neck close. Still, it sounded *too* close.

Forget art.

Retrieving his backpack, he hurried back to the parking lot as fast as the suit allowed. He tripped twice, and swore he heard something following him, but he refused to look back or slow his pace. Drenched with sweat, he reached his car at last. Gravel sprayed up as he sped out of the parking lot.

The next day, he burned the Bigfoot suit.

Mounds
of Trouble

A N OWL HOOTED SOMEWHERE IN THE WOODS. THE SOUND echoed a little, lending it an eerie quality. Jen glanced around but saw no animal eyes glowing in the woods, despite the full moon that shined down from the night sky. Her ears were cold. She pulled her knit cap down over them. Her nose felt like a popsicle, so she cupped one mitten-clad hand over it. She had to be nuts coming out here on Halloween night.

In front of her the earth bulged upward into a mound a hundred feet wide and twenty feet high at its apex. Tall grass and weeds, now dead, cloaked the mound. The moonlight spilled over the earthwork, which had been constructed by human hands a long, long time ago. Jen didn't know exactly when, but she knew it was before European settlers reached the area, before Europeans even heard of Michigan or its Upper Peninsula. So hundreds, maybe thousands, of years after a mysterious race built this mound, here she stood squinting at it in the darkness. Alone.

Something rustled to the left of the mound.

She froze. A vision of wolves pouncing on her flashed through her mind. A chill shimmied down her spine, not entirely due to the temperature.

A figure traipsed out of the shadows.

Jen let out a sigh and relaxed. "What took you so long?"

"Dunno," Eddie said. "Guess the brambles behind the mound slowed me down."

His blond hair seemed to glow in the moonlight, though his face remained in shadow. His backpack appeared as a hump on his back. She wore mittens and a lined fleece jacket; he wore a long-sleeved T-shirt. Jen didn't bother asking him if he was cold, because she knew he'd deny it even if he were. It wasn't cool for a twenty-year-old male to admit such things. Twenty-year-old females, however, could whine about the cold all they wanted.

Not that Jen whined. Jeez, she hoped she didn't anyway.

"What were you looking for back there?" she asked.

"An entrance."

She knew she wouldn't like the answer, but she asked anyway. "Entrance to what?"

"The tomb," he said in a fake spooky voice. "They say the moundbuilders buried their dead in these mounds and that, on All Hallows Eve when the veil between worlds thins, the dead rise to seek their vengeance."

She snorted. "Oh please. They shouldn't let guys take a class in the history of superstitions. They just use the information to try to scare girls."

"Are you scared?"

"Of made-up ghosts? Not likely."

He gave a guttural cackle as he wiggled his fingers in her face. In a really bad imitation of Dracula's voice, he said, "Do not mock the undead."

"I was mocking you, not the undead. Besides, I thought these were ghosts, not vampires."

"Maybe they're ghosts of vampires."

"Vampires are immortal."

Holy mackerel. Now she was debating the difference between vampires and ghosts, while standing at the foot of a big lump in the ground. This had to be the worst date ever. How did she let Eddie convince her to go with him on this idiotic expedition?

She couldn't recall exactly how. It involved lots of flattery and the promise of a scenic drive through the country. Of course, the drive took place in the dark, which kind of negated the whole scenic part of the plan. Even with moonlight, the scenery zipped past as a dark blur.

Dropping his backpack on the ground, Eddie unzipped the main compartment. He brought out a shovel with a folding handle.

"A flashlight would be more useful," she said.

"Nah."

Offering no other explanation, he marched partway up the mound and halted, the unfolded shovel in his right hand. He dropped into a crouch and plunged the shovel into the ground.

A wisp of smoke curled up from beneath the shovel's tip. The wisp floated high into the air, vanishing.

Jen blinked. "What was that?"

"What was what?"

She lowered her gaze from the sky to focus on the mound again. "Nothing."

It must've been nothing, she told herself. A mirage or something. Did mirages happen in the woods, or was that only in the desert?

Whatever. She hadn't really seen anything.

As Eddie proceeded with his excavation, Jen kept an eye on the woods. She had the weirdest feeling that someone or something was watching her. Oh brother. No one was watching except for one very bored owl.

She sucked in a deep breath and let it out slowly. Her breath condensed into a white fog. Duh, of course. The wisp she saw must've been Eddie's breath.

Except it came up from the ground. So much for that theory.

Shuffling closer to Eddie, she peered down at the hole he was digging. The hole measured about two feet in diameter and, so far, a foot deep.

"What are you looking for?" she asked.

"Native artifacts that have magical powers." He paused to glance up at her, no doubt smirking. "I wanna be a shaman, so I can fly and cool stuff like that."

She rolled her eyes. Then a thought occurred to her, a question she now realized she should've asked *before* getting into a car with him. "Is this public land? Do we have permission to be here?"

"Permission has nuances. This is an attractive nuisance, which means we can sue the owner if you trip and sprain your ankle."

"Like I'm taking legal advice from a computer science major." She nudged his leg with the toe of her shoe. "I'm serious. Are we allowed to be here?"

"Technically...no."

"We're trespassing?" She smacked the back of his head. "Oh, you moron! You—"

A howl echoed through the woods.

Jen swallowed hard, but the lump in her throat refused to budge. The howl sounded different than a wolf's, almost like a human. But definitely *not* human. She had no tangible reason for that assessment. She just felt it, deep down, in the place where instinct overrode logic.

Eddie had stopped digging. He twisted his torso to glance backward at the woods where the howl seemed to have originated.

Between the trees, maybe fifty feet away, twin red lights glowed.

Another pair of red lights winked on near the first.

Jen held her breath. She stayed motionless, afraid to even blink.

"What the hell?"

Eddie's exclamation made her jump. Her heart pounding, she said, "Shut up. There's something out there."

"There's something here too."

The quaver in his voice sent a cold wave up her spine. She rotated her head to look at him. He stood in the same spot as before, the shovel held loosely in his hand. As she watched, a white wisp emerged from the hole he'd dug. The mist swirled upward into the heavens, and a second later, another wisp seeped out of the hole.

She seized his arm. "Let's get out of here."

"Yeah."

He grabbed her hand and dragged her off the mound.

Red lights popped on throughout the woods on all sides. The paired lights reminded her of the reflections from animal eyes, though she'd never seen red ones before. And the moonlight seemed insufficient to create such bright reflections.

Something grunted. Another thing grunted in response. Soon, grunts erupted from all sides, even behind the mound.

They were surrounded.

But surrounded by what?

A figure separated from the shadows in the woods. It ambled into the moonlight, halting twenty feet away.

The thing was huge. At least eight feet tall. With unbelievably broad shoulders. Its eyes burned red and a thick coat of hair appeared to cover the body. She could make out no other details.

The creature issued a series of grunts.

Eddie gripped her hand tighter. She sidled closer to him.

The creature let out an ear-piercing wail.

Tendrils of mist swirled down from the sky. The wisps danced around the creature, who held still, his figure as formidable as an Egyptian obelisk.

In the woods, the pairs of red eyes converged on the area behind the creature.

No eyes burned in the woods to the right, the direction she and Eddie had come from, where a narrow trail led back to the road.

Jen bolted for the trees, dragging Eddie behind her. The branch of a pine tree slapped her in the face, but she kept going.

Behind them, a creature screamed.

Their trip back to the car took half the time they'd needed for the hike to the mound. Jen refused to look back until they skidded to a halt beside Eddie's car. Then, she chanced a look.

The woods were dark. Silent.

A jangling drew her attention to Eddie. He held the car keys in one trembling hand. His eyes were wide, the moonlight intensifying the white around his irises. He tried to speak but managed only to stutter a few partial words. Nothing that made much sense.

The blood still thundered behind her eardrums. Goosebumps riddled her skin. Still, she was in better shape than he was.

Jen snatched the keys from him. She ushered him into the car, then circled around to the driver's door and climbed in. As

she steered the car through a U-turn, she glanced into the woods. Nothing there.

Half a mile down the road, a flash of movement in the sky caught her attention. She turned her eyes toward the movement. A snakelike wisp of fog drifted over the road, high above, disappearing behind the treetops on the opposite side.

She saw nothing else for the remainder of the drive. By the time they reached her apartment building, Eddie had recovered enough to drive himself home. As she climbed out of the car, he asked, "When can I see you again?"

Jen stared at him. "When pigs fly, hell freezes over, and politicians stop lying."

She slammed the car door shut.

The Locked
Barn Mystery

ROGER HAD A GHOST IN HIS BARN. IT WAS THE ONLY EXPLA-
nation, but it was utter nonsense. Ghosts did not exist, therefore
he could not blame a spectral visitor for what happened.

For what kept happening.

Roger stood just outside the barn door, watching as his two horses,
Patty and Bobby, ambled out of the barn. Patty, the mare, was a golden
palomino with a white mane and tail. Bobby, the gelding, sported a
reddish-brown coat that glowed with a copper sheen in the morning
sun. As they made their way out into the field, the horses paid little
attention to Roger—since he'd already fed them, fulfilling his purpose
for the morning. Sure, they liked him. But the lure of the open pasture
beckoned to them now.

Bobby shook his head, gave a little buck, and took off across the
field. Patty raced after him.

Roger shut the barn door, and the latch fell into place with a
snap. Anyone could open the latch, which meant anyone could
sneak into the barn. Maybe somebody was playing a weird trick
on him. Why, he must ask himself, and he had no answer for the
question. Besides, he found no footprints to indicate that anyone

approached the barn, except for him. Of course, his boots rarely impressed their tread into the ground unless a good rain had fallen in the last couple days, transforming the earth into sticky slop.

Somebody was messing with his horses. And he didn't like it one bit.

Out in the field, Patty and Bobby were grazing. Every so often Bobby lifted his head to grab ahold of Patty's tail. She'd kick at him with one back foot, a halfhearted attempt at scolding. Bobby would relinquish his hold on her tail, and the two would then return to grazing.

Roger leaned against the barn. Three times in the past month it had happened, always overnight. In the morning, the horses always acted excited—just like this morning—as if something either really fun or rather scary transpired the previous night. Something that left no trace, other than the thing that seemed to be the point of the exercise. The thing he always found. The thing that was...weird.

In all his years of owning horses, he'd never seen anything like it. Even after three occurrences, he still couldn't stand to think about it. He tried not to picture it in his mind. Tried not to name it. Definitely, he told no one about it.

He had a ghost in his barn. Nothing else could create such a thing without leaving any tracks.

Roger raked a hand through his hair. He was old enough to know better than to blame ghosts but young enough that, if he told anyone about the incidents, they'd label him crazy rather than eccentric. Crazy got people locked up. Eccentric made them loveable. If he had money, he might qualify as eccentric despite his age. Unfortunately, he didn't have enough money to buy his way into eccentric territory.

Back to the house then.

That night, Roger locked the horses in the barn as usual. With a pack of wolves roaming the area, keeping the horses in overnight seemed prudent. Wolves could take down moose, after all. If they got hungry enough, they might go after a horse. Two nights ago, he heard a wolf howling close by, probably at the far end of the five-acre field. Too close for Roger's comfort.

Too bad he couldn't blame the wolves for the other thing.

Patty went into the barn first, as usual. She was settling in to munch on hay by the time Bobby trotted up to the barn. Something out in the woods had distracted the gelding since after Roger fed the horses their afternoon meal. All evening, every time Roger glanced out the window he saw Bobby standing near the edge of the field, staring into the woods. The gelding stood with his head up, ears forward, intent on whatever he saw or heard.

Bobby slowed to a walk. He paused to nuzzle Roger's hand, then headed inside the barn to join Patty at the hay. The pair munched happily on their snack.

Overhead, a full moon drowned out the twinkling of all but the brightest stars. A single cloud, narrow and wispy, scudded across the moon.

Roger sighed. In the moonlight, he watched his breath condense into a cloud and gradually dissipate. He pulled his jacket tighter around himself, shoving his hands into the pockets. The weatherman said it might snow tonight, though an inch at most was expected.

Tonight, he'd come prepared. No more stealth entries into the barn. One door led into and out of the structure. He intended to make certain nobody got inside tonight.

From his pocket he retrieved a padlock. It was old but still in good condition. He'd even managed to find the key for the padlock, despite having left it in the infamous "safe place" years ago. Now he hooked the padlock onto the door latch and clicked it shut.

No trespassers tonight.

Unless they could jump eighteen feet in the air.

Roger glanced up at the hay loft door. It stood eighteen feet off the ground, with no ladder or tree nearby to allow access. The only way to get into the loft was to climb the ladder inside the barn, which he'd just locked up tight, or to leap the eighteen feet.

Satisfied with the security of the barn, Roger strolled back to the house and went to bed.

The next morning, he marched out to the barn and unlocked

the door. As he slipped the padlock into his pocket, he swung the door open.

Patty was lying down amid the leftover hay. She lifted her head to gaze at him with a sleepy expression.

To the rear of Patty, partially hidden by her bulk, Bobby nibbled at the hay.

Roger walked toward the little stall he used as a storage room.

Patty jumped to her feet. Her mane billowed.

Halfway through the stall door, Roger froze. He'd only seen it peripherally, but he knew he had seen it. The thing was back.

He needed to be sure.

Shutting the stall door, he strode toward the mare. She tossed her head up and backed away from him. Ears up, she watched him. He took another step closer. She raised her head high but didn't move.

Bobby observed from a dozen feet away. Roger swerved in the gelding's direction, stretching out a hand to pat his nose. Just as Roger's fingertips grazed Bobby's nose, the horse ducked his head away.

This was not how horses normally acted. However, this was how they'd acted the other three times the thing appeared.

Roger snatched up a handful of hay. As he stretched out his hand palm up to Patty, offering her the hay, he took slow steps toward her. She sniffed the hay in his hand. He reached up with his free hand to rub her forehead. She started to toss her head, but apparently thought better of it. Lowering her head again, she took the hay from his palm and began to munch on it.

Murmuring soothing words, Roger scratched behind her ear. Then he patted her neck as he inched his way past her head. Bobby ambled over to nuzzle his companion, which distracted Patty enough that Roger could examine her mane.

There it was. Identical to the previous ones.

Roger brushed aside strands of mane that had fallen over the thing. He slid his hand under it, lifting it up into the light.

Two thick locks of mane hair had each been twisted to form twin ropes. About halfway down the ropes, the two had been woven together into a tight braid. The end of the braid was looped upward and tucked into the braid itself. Roger knew from past experience that the only way to remove the braid was to cut it out of the mane.

He lifted the braid higher, bending forward to study it more closely. The braid featured a weave so tight and complicated that he wondered how anyone could fashion such a thing. A lock of three or four strands appeared to have been separated from and woven around the rest of the braid, creating a kind of basket weave pattern around the outside of the braid. He'd never seen anything like it.

Dropping the braid, Roger ducked under Patty's neck. Bobby stood right in front of Roger now, but Bobby's mane was on the other side of his neck. Bobby twisted his head to the side, trying to rub his face on Roger's shirt. The gelding pushed hard enough that Roger stumbled backward a step.

He pushed Bobby's head away and patted the gelding's neck. He knew Bobby didn't mean to hurt him. He just got a little too friendly sometimes, especially when he was excited, like both the horses were this morning. Whatever happened last night, it got them agitated.

Roger moved around Bobby's head to the other side of the horse's neck. He sifted through the mane with his fingers but found nothing. On the other three occasions, the same thing happened. He found a braid in one horse's mane, but not the other's. Whoever the perpetrators were, they never braided both horses' manes, maybe because weaving one incredibly complex braid took so long that they didn't want to waste more time creating a second braid.

He assumed there was more than one perpetrator. Accomplishing the task must've required at least two people—one to hold the horse, another to braid the mane.

Why would anyone break into his barn just to play with his horses' manes?

Except they didn't break in. Roger shoved his hand into his coat pocket, feeling the padlock tucked inside it. The door had been securely closed and no one messed with the padlock.

Bobby nickered.

"Yeah, I know," Roger said. "You want your breakfast."

The gelding nickered again, as if responding in the affirmative.

Roger strode back to the stall. He scooped oats out of a big bag, dumping some into each of two plastic buckets. He carried the buckets to the horses and set them on the ground about a dozen feet apart.

Bobby headed straight for one bucket, and Patty made a beeline for the other. When Patty dropped her head to shove her nose into the bucket, the braid in her mane flopped into view again.

The hairs on the back of Roger's neck stiffened. A faint chill whispered down his spine.

How did someone get into the barn?

He rubbed his neck, frowning.

While the horses crunched on their oats, Roger wandered outside. Hands in his coat pockets, he stared up at the hay loft door. It was the only way into the barn, aside from the locked door. No one jimmied the lock, therefore the perpetrators must've entered through the hay loft. But how did they get up there?

He searched the ground. The constant horse traffic going into and coming out of the barn had worn the earth bare. Morning dew had softened the ground so that his boots left the faintest of tracks. Though he searched in what he deemed a slow and methodical manner, scrutinizing the ground with each step, he found nothing other than the imprints of hooves and his own boots.

A ladder should've left sharp impressions in the ground. He saw none. Somehow the perpetrators got up into the loft without a ladder and without leaving any footprints.

Unless they didn't enter through the loft.

Well, how else could they get into the barn?

He knew of one way to find out for sure. He'd sit in that damn hay loft all night every night until he finally caught the buggers. Or until he went insane from lack of sleep. Maybe he was already insane, thinking somebody magically snuck into a locked barn and braided his horse's mane. The braids might be simple tangles.

No. He couldn't convince himself of that. After a lifetime living with horses, he knew the tangles they got from their daily excursions into the woods looked nothing like the complex braids that had shown up in their manes lately. Tangles looked like...tangles. They didn't have intricately woven ropes of hair. No explanation made sense unless he accepted that someone or something braided the horses' manes on purpose.

Tonight he'd catch the miscreants. One way or the other.

Shortly after dark, he crept out to the barn as if he were the miscreant conducting a nighttime raid on the barn. Although he brought a flashlight with him, he navigated by moonlight to increase his stealth. His dark clothing and ski mask concealed his pale skin, which looked paler by moonlight. In one hand he toted the flashlight, and in the other he carried his .357 revolver. Anyone who stole into his barn in the dark of night, intent on messing with his horses, posed a potential threat. He subscribed to the better-safe-than-sorry mentality.

He'd left the barn door latched but not secured with the padlock. He wanted to lock the door, to find out how the intruders got inside without breaking the lock, but he could only secure the door from the outside. The door opened inward, however, so earlier this evening—when he locked the horses in for the night—he'd lugged several cement blocks into the barn. The blocks were left behind by the guy who owned this property before Roger. For a dozen years, the cement blocks sat behind the barn, in an area outside the fenced-in pasture for the horses. Roger kept thinking he'd use the blocks for something, but he never did. Until tonight.

Now he let himself into the barn, shutting the door after himself. He heard the latch click into place. The horses, busily munching on hay, glanced up at him. Disinterested, they resumed eating.

Next, Roger hauled the cement blocks over to the door. By stacking them right up against the door, he managed to barricade it rather nicely. Only a he-man could shove the door open now. The intruders would have to come in through the hay loft—and he couldn't wait to see how they pulled off that stunt.

He climbed up to the loft, shifted a few hay bales to make a nice little hideout for himself, and settled in for the duration. Occasionally, he risked hitting the button on his digital watch that lit up the face. Time seemed to crawl by, and eventually he stopped check-ing his watch. He set the revolver on the floor. The flashlight he laid across his lap. His eyelids felt heavier and heavier. They fluttered shut, and he felt his head loll to the right.

Whump.

Roger woke with a jerk. His heart pounded. Moving only his eyes, he scanned the loft.

Over the top of the hay he spied a humanlike figure standing near the loft door.

Roger held still. Shadows cloaked the figure. In spite of the lighting, Roger knew instantly this was no teenager playing a prank. The intruder was huge, at least two feet taller than Roger, who considered himself a big guy. The intruder sported wide shoulders and a thick neck. The guy's arms looked massive too. And his torso did not narrow at the waist. Jeez, was this guy a steroid addict or what?

Turning sideways to Roger, the intruder faced the interior of the barn. He could probably glimpse the horses down below, if only as silhouettes in the gloom.

Slowly, cautiously, Roger picked up the revolver. It made a little scritch noise as he lifted it off the wood floor.

The intruder whipped his head around to stare in Roger's direction.

Roger froze. He didn't even breathe.

The intruder lifted his chin. The action reminded Roger of a dog sniffing the air. People didn't sniff the air, though, at least not any of the people Roger knew.

Giving a quick nod, as if satisfied, the intruder lumbered to the loft's edge, where it overlooked the interior of the barn. Lumbered seemed the most appropriate term for the intruder's gait. Despite the apparent inelegance of his motions, the intruder made no sound as he trod across the floorboards.

Roger inhaled a cautious breath, then let it out with equal care. Since even he couldn't hear the whispering of his breaths, he hoped the sound was inaudible to the linebacker across the hay from him too.

Linebacker? Roger silently scoffed at his own word choice. This guy probably clobbered entire teams of linebackers and sumo wrestlers all by himself.

The intruder peered over the loft's rim. Then he sidled to the left a few paces, edging nearer to the ladder. Roger waited for the guy to clamber down the wooden rungs.

Instead, the intruder leaped off the loft.

Roger stared at the spot where the guy had stood. A soft whump signaled the intruder had touched down in the barn below.

The guy leaped eighteen feet to the ground.

More astonishing yet, the guy must've leaped *up* an equal distance to get inside the loft.

Every hair on Roger's body stiffened. Rising into a crouch, he grasped the gun tighter in his right hand. He wielded the flashlight in his left hand, one finger poised over the power button. Thus armed, he crept toward the loft's rim and peeked down into the barn.

The intruder held out a hand to Bobby. The gelding tossed his head up, eyes wide. The intruder opened his hand, offering something to the horse. Bobby huffed a breath out his nose, tossing his head. The intruder waited, hand still outstretched. After a moment, Bobby craned his neck to sniff the intruder's hand. And then he took whatever the intruder held.

Crunch, crunch.

It sounded like Bobby was eating an apple. Roger stared down at the scene. Apple trees grew wild in the woods, so the intruder could've snagged the fruit on his way here.

A scuffling sound erupted outside the barn. The noise was soft, yet distinct. Something was moving around outside.

Down below, the intruder fingered Bobby's mane. Getting ready to braid it, no doubt.

The scuffling outside stopped. Something grunted.

The noise came from outside, just like the scuffling.

Roger waddled away from the loft's edge and risked getting to his feet. Holding the gun at his side, aimed at the floor, he trotted on tiptoes to the loft door. Once there, he flattened his body against

the wall beside the opening and bent his head forward just far enough to let him peek outside. Eighteen feet below him, three figures loitered. Two of the figures seemed to be hoisting the third into the air.

All three appeared as stocky and powerful as the intruder currently fondling his horse's mane.

A shiver rattled his body. He sucked in a breath, swung the flashlight in front of his body, aimed the light downward, and punched the power button.

Light showered the figures. One creature, clearly smaller than others, stood on the shoulders of his larger buddy as he apparently prepared to leap for the loft door. All three creatures threw back their heads to squint into the brilliance of Roger's flashlight beam.

Creatures. Roger didn't know what else to call them. Except maybe...

Bigfoot. Sasquatch. Yeti.

Didn't Yetis live in the Himalayas? These must be Bigfoots. Bigfeet. Whatever. They were hair covered and definitely not human, but not apes either. Something in between. Ape-men. Man-apes.

Creatures. Things.

The creature standing on the other one's shoulders jumped off onto the ground. One of them shrieked.

Roger winced. Jeez, that thing had lungs as powerful as its muscles.

A grunt issued from behind him, from down in the barn. One of the horses nickered.

First Roger heard the horse hooves clomping. A swishing sound followed.

Whump.

The loft shook. Roger dropped the flashlight, which tumbled out the loft door.

Oh hell.

He turned, flattening his back against the wall. The creature straightened, having just landed in the loft. The beast grunted softly, canting its head to eye Roger.

Outside, footfalls thwapped. The other creatures were running away, Roger assumed.

The creature before him grunted again.

Then it ran for the loft door. In two huge strides, the creature crossed the distance and hurled itself out the door. A whump followed. Footfalls thwapped.

After a moment, the sound of the creatures' flight faded into silence.

Rustling noises emanated from the barn below. The horses were restless.

He didn't blame them.

Leaning sideways, Roger poked his head out the loft door. His flashlight lay on the ground, its beam splaying across the ground.

For several minutes, he stood there. Motionless. Silent. Unable to think except to remind himself to breathe.

Finally, he climbed down the ladder into the barn. After assuring himself the horses were fine, despite the half-finished braid in Bobby's mane, he exited the barn. He didn't bother to lock the door.

He retrieved the flashlight and went back to the house. Though he tried to get some sleep, the thoughts spinning in his brain refused to let him relax. At dawn, he headed back out to the barn.

By the light of sunrise, he hunted for tracks in the earth. He saw none but the imprints of his own boots.

Then he realized his mistake. He'd been looking for shoe prints. The creatures wore no shoes, as far as he could tell.

Once he adjusted his assumptions, he spotted the tracks. They were vague impressions, similar to a bare human foot but without the arch. The footprints impressed lightly in the earth. No wonder he missed them before. He had to be looking for the faint impressions of bare feet in order to spot them.

He had to be looking for Bigfoot tracks.

After that morning, Roger stopped looking for tracks around the barn. He stopped locking the barn door. No locks would keep out the creatures. They must've entered via the loft because they preferred to, not because the padlock intimidated them. He doubted much intimidated them. They must've liked jumping into the loft. Maybe they thought it was fun. Maybe they liked making Roger scratch his head in puzzlement.

Every so often, he found a braid in the mane of one of the horses. He stopped examining the braids closely. If the creatures wanted to braid his horses' manes occasionally, he had no choice but to let them. They seemed to mean no harm by it. So he avoided thinking about it.

And he never told a soul what he saw that night.

Nobody would believe him anyway.

A Trace of Bigfoot

CHARLIE SHUT THE DOOR AND LEANED AGAINST THE pickup. He gazed out at the woods, inhaling the scent of pine and damp earth. It had been too long since his last visit to the real woods. As much as he loved teaching history, every few weeks he needed to leave the university behind and reacquaint himself with the outdoors. It amazed him that he could live amid the Northern Michigan woods yet rarely experience the wilderness.

The trees, mostly evergreens interspersed with hardwoods, towered eighty feet overhead. Directly above the two-track road, a strip of blue sky was visible. Up ahead, the road disappeared into the trees. Deeper into the forest, a woodpecker hammered on a hollow tree and a mourning dove cooed.

Footsteps crunched on gravel behind him. Charlie turned to the man approaching him, a burly middle-aged fellow with a goatee. Steve Johansson halted about eight feet away from Charlie, halfway between his own pickup Charlie's. A touch of fear showed in his eyes as he looked at Charlie without meeting the other man's gaze.

"That's where it started," Johansson said. He waved an unsteady hand at the region where the shadows of the trees swallowed the road. "It was no bear or nothing like that. I couldn't see it real clear but I'm sure. I think it was..." Johansson ducked his head and shoved his hands in his jeans pockets. "I think it was Bigfoot."

Charlie glanced through the open window of his pickup into the cab. His son leaned forward against his seatbelt to watch Steve Johansson through the windshield. He must've heard the older man's words, because a smirk warped his lips. Johansson seemed unaware of the teenage boy eyeing him with derision.

A gust of wind rattled the trees. Johansson jerked his head up and fixed his wide eyes on the woods.

Charlie reached into the pickup's bed and grabbed ahold of his backpack. Hefting it onto his shoulders, he told Johansson, "Show me where you found the tracks and then you can leave."

Johansson shook his head. His face went pale. "I won't go in there. Never again. If you saw that thing, you wouldn't want to either."

"Just show me the tracks. That's all I'm asking."

Johansson had balked when Charlie suggested returning to the scene. He didn't like talking about it, period. When the doorbell had rung at seven o'clock last night, Charlie opened the door to find his neighbor, Steve Johansson, standing there with a look of absolute terror on his face. He'd seen something in the woods that day while hunting, something drastically abnormal. He begged Charlie to help him.

"What can I do?" Charlie had asked.

"Show me I'm not crazy," Johansson replied. "Or show me I'm wrong. Don't care which."

Charlie knew he should say no but he just couldn't. Johansson wanted answers. And in the five years Charlie had known him, he never seemed like the type of fellow who would hallucinate or lie about seeing a seven-foot-tall, hairy creature that walked upright like a human being.

"Okay." Johansson trudged past Charlie toward the woods. "I'll show you."

A voice from inside the pickup said, "This is lame."

"You wanted to come along," Charlie said to his son, "so get off your duff. And this is not lame."

As his son climbed out of the pickup, Charlie pulled the compass out of his jacket pocket. Johansson had stopped at the edge of the woods on the left side of the road, 30 feet away.

Ricky slammed the passenger door. The pickup rocked. Charlie glanced at his son, who held his backpack slung over one shoulder. The pack sagged at the bottom, weighed down by its contents.

"How many books did you bring, Ricky?" Charlie asked.

"Dad," the boy whined. "I told you my name's Rick. Only babies are called Ricky."

"Sorry, I forgot."

Charlie led his son to Johansson, and the threesome headed into the woods down a deer trail that was invisible from the road. The trail snaked through brush and grass for about a hundred feet, then opened out onto the rocky shores of a small stream.

Johansson halted. He pointed at the opposite shore. "There."

Charlie hopped across the stream in two steps. Pausing there, he surveyed the ground for the imprints Johansson said he'd found. At first, he saw nothing. Then, a shape popped out at him.

Ricky bounded across the stream. Charlie flung a hand out to stop him. The boy stumbled backward, falling onto his butt in the water. "Dad!"

"You were about to destroy the evidence."

Charlie knelt by the tracks. They were impressed deeply into the soil. Their shape resembled a human foot, except for the lack of an arch—and the size. He set his foot down next to the nearest print. It was twice as long as his boot.

Ricky sat forward on his knees, bending forward to scrutinize the track. "Is that supposed to be a Sasquatch footprint? It looks fake."

Charlie glanced at Johansson. The man either hadn't heard Ricky or didn't care what a teenage boy thought.

Did Bigfoot exist? Five years ago, Charlie would've answered with an emphatic no. Today, he wasn't so sure. He'd read articles and books about Bigfoot, written by anthropologists, that presented

some damn convincing physical evidence that, coupled with eyewitness testimony, seemed hard to deny.

Problem was, like those anthropologists who dared talk about Bigfoot, Charlie knew he was risking his career by doing this. If anyone at the university found out, he could kiss tenure goodbye. His tenure review was in progress, and he'd already skated out onto thin ice with the last paper he published. Writing about the history of wild man lore seemed innocent enough, but his blasted subconscious convinced him to include two sentences at the end of the paper, sentences that mentioned Bigfoot and suggested perhaps the long-running legends of hairy wild men were based on sightings of Bigfoot-type creatures.

A whoop pierced the silence.

Charlie froze. Ee-yoop, the sound came again. In the distance, other voices answered with overlapping ee-yoops. What the hell?

Johansson bolted down the deer trail, crashing through the brush on his way back to his vehicle. In a moment, his footfalls faded and the silence returned.

Charlie's heart pounded. Half-formed thoughts ricocheted inside his brain. He had never heard a sound like that before, not in all his years in the woods.

"What was that?" Ricky asked. "A wolf?"

Charlie said nothing. Ricky clambered to his feet. They stood still for a minute or two, but no cries whooped through the woods. No animals traipsed out of the woods.

"Can we go now?" Ricky asked.

"Not yet." Charlie studied the five-toed tracks. With his gaze he traced them up the shoreline a half dozen feet, where they angled right toward the woods. Should he follow the trail? What might await him at the end?

Was he ready to learn the answers?

One way to find out. He marched down the shore, paralleling the tracks. Ricky clomped after him. They followed the trail of footprints as it ducked into the trees, but a few feet in Charlie lost the trail. Backtracking didn't help. The footprints had vanished into the grass and weeds.

Charlie considered his options. He had none, really. This wasn't his forte—tracking mysterious animals science said couldn't exist.

With a sigh, Charlie said, "We can go now."

A few minutes later, they piled into the pickup. Charlie started the engine, executed a U-turn, and paused the pickup alongside the deer trail.

Inside the woods, a shadow shifted.

Charlie squinted, leaned his head out the window.

The dark shape stepped into a wedge of sunlight. It turned its head toward Charlie, meeting his gaze for a split second, then stepped into the shadows again, disappearing from sight.

"Dad, are you having a stroke or what?"

Charlie blinked. Looked at his son. And then he drove off down the road. Only after he got home did he realize what he'd done. He'd stared a Bigfoot in the face.

He couldn't tell anyone, if he wanted to keep his job. Not that anyone would believe him. Well, one person would. And that somebody knew how to keep a secret.

Charlie got back in his pickup and drove to Steve Johansson's place.

A Stone's Throw
from Bigfoot

PUFFY WHITE CLOUDS SKIDDED ACROSS THE SKY, BORNE on a high-level wind. Katy watched the clouds for a moment, then turned her attention to the valley below, a swathe of green grass studded with multicolored wildflowers. From her perch on the mountainside, leaning against a tree trunk, Katy could see the entire valley and the passes on either side through which a distant freeway carved a path. A smog bank edged up the northern pass and the flanking mountains, heading toward the town nestled in the valley's center.

Katy sighed. She thought going to college in California would be exciting, but instead she discovered the joys of breathing smog and battling traffic jams. Her weekend escapes to the mountains saved her sanity. She missed the wilderness back home. The trouble with weekend hikes, though, was that she always ran into other people on the trails. Today, she'd seen at least three dozen cars in the parking lot at the trailhead.

Rain the previous night left the ground damp and dotted with puddles. Katy turned and hopped over a small puddle to get back on the trail. School had gone okay this week, with one exception. Normally, she kept her wacky thoughts to herself because she realized teachers, whether in high school or in college, disliked the kinds of questions she asked. But during her ancient history class, when the professor proclaimed the Great Pyramid of Giza to be a tomb, her hand seemed to rise on its own. When the professor acknowledged her, she asked politely, "If the Great Pyramid was a tomb, why haven't any human remains or funerary equipment ever been found inside it?"

The professor aimed a condescending smile at her. "The tomb was robbed in ancient times."

Before she could ask a follow-up question, the professor launched back into his lecture. Her courage abandoned her then, though the questions kept popping into her brain. Other Egyptian tombs had been robbed, yet some bit of something always remained for modern archaeologists to find. The Great Pyramid was utterly empty. A lot of ancient history, the way she'd learned it in school, made no sense.

Thunk.

The sound came from her left. She glanced that way. A fist-size rock lay on the ground a dozen feet away, on top of the grass. She'd walked right over that spot on her way to the tree, and no rock lay there when she passed the area. The thunk might've been a stone hitting the ground. Did someone throw a rock at her?

She surveyed the area around her, peering into the trees, studying every shadow. No silhouettes jumped out at her. Nothing suggested another living thing loitered within proximity to her. Although a squirrel might hide in one of the trees, she doubted a squirrel could pick up a rock that size, much less hurl it at her. She must've stepped over the rock without noticing it.

Hefting her backpack onto her shoulders, Katy started off down the trail again. A lonely hike in the woods could make anyone imagine things. Though she never thought of herself as prone to delusions, maybe everyone else was right about her. Maybe she was crazy. Her interest in the paranormal, her inability to accept the mainstream story about ancient history, her willingness to fully explore the nuttiest of ideas just in case it contained some kernel of

truth—these tendencies drove other people to label her too crazy to deal with.

The trail curved to follow the mountain's topography. A patch of wildflowers came into view alongside the trail. She squatted beside them and stretched a hand out to finger the blossoms. They were saucer shaped, blue with white centers. Lovely, she thought.

Thunk.

A rock landed on the ground to her right, inches from her boot. It had come from straight ahead, up the mountainside above her. She tilted her head back to gaze into the shadows of the firs, oaks, and pines. One shadow seemed out of place. She squinted at it. Was that a human silhouette?

Katy snaked a hand behind her to unzip the side pocket of her backpack. As she slid her hand into the pocket, closing her fingers around the hilt of her knife, the silhouette ducked behind a thick pine tree. Pulling out the knife, she jumped up and hopped sideways, but she couldn't find the silhouette again. Whatever it was, it had gone away.

A shiver rattled her spine. She glanced down at the knife in her hand. What did she expect to do with this? If a psycho was stalking her through the forest, then a four-inch knife would offer her little protection. Still, it seemed better than nothing. Knife gripped in her fist, she headed back the way she'd come, her exploratory urge summarily quashed. She wanted to get out of here.

A shadow scared her into rushing back to her car? What kind of wimp was she? The kind with half a brain, she decided, a trait that might keep her alive. She trusted her instincts. And right now they were telling her to get the hell out of there.

She rounded the curve and froze. A man was ambling toward her. He looked about forty, with salt-and-pepper hair. He carried a leather backpack slung over one shoulder, clutching its strap in one hand, while in the other hand he grasped a black object. A cowboy hat dipped low over his forehead. He wore camouflage pants and a matching T-shirt emblazoned with some kind of logo. Catching sight of her, the man halted. He reached up to grab hold of his backpack strap with his free hand. A slight smile played at his lips. "Well, hey there."

He spoke with a Texas drawl. She eyed him with curiosity but kept her distance.

The man said, "You seen or heard anythin' strange out here?"

She stiffened. "Why do you ask?"

"You have, I can tell."

He took two steps closer. She saw now that his T-shirt logo incorporated a humanlike silhouette that partially blended into the letter S beside it. The rest of the logo spelled out, in highly stylized lettering, the letters "quatch this". The logo said "squatch this," which sounded like nonsense words.

The man said, "I'm huntin' for monsters out here, and you've got the look of someone who spotted one. You're pale as a ghost, hon."

She glanced over her shoulder toward the area she'd just left. Facing the man again, she said, "No, *hon*. I didn't see anything. Sorry to disappoint you."

His slight smile morphed into a smirk. He shrugged.

The hairs on the back of her neck bristled. She felt someone watching her, someone other than the smirking cowboy. She wanted to run for the parking lot, even though she knew it lay half a mile down the trail, but she did not want to flee past the cowboy. He might be in cahoots with the figure stalking her from the shadows.

Jeez, she was paranoid. With good reason. Out the corner of her eye, she spotted the silhouette in the trees higher up the mountainside.

The cowboy gestured at her knife. "That ain't gonna do you much good. These monsters are stronger than Hercules and they turn mean in a flash."

"What monsters?"

"The kind you don't want to tick off. Squatches, we call 'em."

"I don't know what you're talking about and I don't care. Please leave me alone."

Crack. The sound of a twig snapping somewhere up the slope. Katy rotated her torso to look into the trees. She couldn't see the silhouette.

The cowboy walked to her, set down his pack, and held out his hand to offer her the black object he carried. It was a mini-cassette recorder. He pressed the record button and said, "Hold this for a sec."

She hesitated, then took the recorder. He strode closer to the slope. Tilting his head back, he cupped his hands around his mouth like a megaphone and whooped so loud she winced. He whooped twice more, then lowered his hands and waited, gaze fixed on the woods.

Katy vacillated between watching the cowboy and searching the shadows between the trees, in the area where she last saw the silhouette. Silence reigned. No birds tweeted, no insects chirped, nothing at all seemed to be alive except for the two of them.

After a few minutes, the cowboy sagged his shoulders and returned to her side. He took back the recorder and punched the stop button. His smirk was gone, replaced by a pinched expression.

"Damn," he said. "It usually works."

"Works for what?"

He backed away from her, focused on rewinding the tape in his recorder. She waited another minute, but when he said nothing else, she asked, "What on earth were you trying to accomplish?"

Shrugging, he snatched up his backpack. She swore he blushed, briefly, before he regained his composure to meet her gaze.

"Just tryin' to impress a pretty girl," he said. "See ya 'round, hon."

He marched off down the trail, nodding as he passed her. She turned to watch him amble away, the backpack dangling from his fist. That was when she saw the lettering on the back of his T-shirt. It read "Sasquatch Hunter." Suddenly, the words on the front of his shirt made sense. "Squatch" must refer to Sasquatch, the legendary bipedal monster said to roam the forests of the West Coast. "Squatch this" must be a play on words then, a pun based on the phrase "watch this." The cowboy liked dumb jokes.

Katy kept an eye on the man until he receded out of sight, then she headed out in the opposite direction. Minutes ticked by. The feeling of being watched returned, so she quickened her pace into a near trot.

Thunk. A rock sailed out of the trees to plop onto the trail in front of her. Katy hopped to a stop. The toe of her boot bumped the rock. She glanced around but saw nothing. No silhouette. No cowboy. The rock had come from the woods to her left, and she doubted the cowboy could've doubled back through the woods so quickly without making a ruckus. She picked up the rock, rolled it in her hand. Lots of hikers in the woods today. Any one of them might've tossed rocks at her as a prank.

Goosebumps prickled her skin. She looked down at the spot where the rock had landed. Sweeping her gaze rightward from that spot, she froze. Gulped. Blinked. It was still there. An imprint in the damp soil. The print looked humanoid, yet it lacked an arch and measured longer and wider than her own boot. The print impressed the soil deeply too, far deeper than any human footprint she'd seen.

This couldn't be. It sure looked like it, though. A Bigfoot footprint.

Katy leaned over the print. Sure, she believed such things might exist but—

A sneaker-clad foot stamped down on the track.

Katy jerked her head up. A teenage boy bounded backward away from her. He muttered, "Sorry, ma'am."

Three other teenagers darted up the trail past her. She must've gotten so lost in her thoughts about the imprint that she failed to notice the marauding teens. They continued down the trail. The boy had nearly run over her.

She looked down at the imprint. The teenager's sneaker track obliterated it.

Katy rose. Maybe the imprint hadn't been foot shaped. It might've been nothing at all, the humanoid shape an artifact of her paranoid imagination reacting to the cowboy's suggestion of monsters in the woods. Then there was the Sasquatch logo on his shirt. Subconscious hints that her mind may have elaborated on a bit too much.

Had her mind created a Bigfoot track out of a natural depression or a human footprint eroded by the rains? Even if it had, she still couldn't explain the silhouette in the woods.

Maybe the cowboy was right. There were monsters out here.

Either way, she might never know for certain. Add another mystery to her list of things she needed to explore. One day she just might tackle those mysteries, one by one. Not today.

Katy trudged back to the parking lot.

Wild Men in the Woods

A RAVEN SWOOPED LOW OVER THE FOREST. RICK WATCHED it through an opening in the trees overhead. The birds seemed to be keeping tabs on them today. Maybe the birds were laughing at the two dumb humans prowling through the woods below, engaged in a futile search for the woodland equivalent of a ghost.

The whole idea was stupid. Rick dropped his backpack on the ground and leaned back against the tree behind him. His denim jacket scraped on the bark. He couldn't believe he was out here. He couldn't believe he'd let his father convince him to spend his spring break in the woods hunting for Bigfoot, with nothing to eat except granola bars, ham sandwiches, and beef jerky. At eight o'clock each morning, they piled into Dad's truck and drove to a spot in the woods, a different spot each day, then set out on a ridiculous quest to find hairy monsters that some lunatic or other claimed to have seen in the area. They searched until sunset, when they wood pile back into Dad's truck and headed home.

At first Rick thought it was kind of fun. He liked the woods, and it was a nice break from his college classes. By the third day, however, he'd gotten mightily sick of ham sandwiches and beef jerky. At least he could still stomach the granola bars.

He shifted position. His jacket raked across the bark with a loud *scritch*.

A hand seized his upper arm. He glanced at his father, whose fingers tightened on his arm. Dad frowned at him. "Are you trying to scare off every living thing within a mile of us?"

"No."

"Stealth," he said, releasing Rick's arm. "That's the name of the game. We're hunting elusive creatures, Ricky, so try to be a little more careful."

"My name is Rick. Not Ricky, not Richie, not—"

"All right, all right. I'll try to remember. But I called you Ricky for fifteen years, so it may take time for me to get used to it."

Rick pushed away from the tree and straightened. He looked down at his father, who was five inches shorter. "You've had six years to get used to it. How much longer do you need?"

His father shrugged.

Rick lifted the backpack onto his shoulders, fastening the strap around his waist. Dad trudged away from him, and he followed. His stomach grumbled. He glanced at his watch, which gave the time as two-fifteen. Only two hours since lunch, and already he felt hungry enough to gnaw the bark off a tree. Well, maybe not quite that hungry—yet.

Through the woods they marched, like a tiny army chasing an invisible enemy, or in this case, an enemy that didn't exist. Rick tested his knowledge of the trees as they slogged onward. Dad had taught him how to recognize most of the native trees, but his classes left him little time to practice the skill. On this trip, he had nothing but time.

He surveyed the woods. There was a maple, one of the easiest to spot due to its distinctive leaves. Next he spotted an aspen, with its heart-shaped leaves. Firs and spruces confused him because they looked similar, both being evergreens with shorter needles than the ones on pine trees. He paused to examine the needles on one evergreen. Fir or spruce?

Crack.

Rick jerked upright at the sound. Something had snapped a twig or small branch. Twenty feet away, his father stood frozen, gaze scanning the woods. Rick tiptoed to his father.

"What is it?" Rick whispered.

"Something's watching us."

"How do you know?"

Dad nodded to the left. Rick tracked his father's gaze into the trees, past a stand of maples, to an area where the boughs of a large pine sheltered a small clearing. He saw nothing there, except trees and grass and a smattering of wildflowers.

His father spoke in a voice so soft Rick could barely hear it. "I think one of them is watching."

Rick crinkled his eyebrows. "One of who?"

"A forest ape."

"You mean Bigfoot."

"Yes, Rick, I mean Bigfoot."

Rick snorted. "You really think these monsters are spying on us? What are you waiting for, one of them to jump out and yell boo? If you can see one, why not go over there and—"

"I can't see them," Dad said in a patient tone he must've perfected in his teaching. "Something broke a twig. And don't you smell that?"

"No."

"Take a good whiff."

Rolling his eyes, Rick sniffed. And stiffened. He did smell something. He sniffed again, drawing in more air. It stank like rotten eggs and spoiled meat. "Smells like a dead animal."

Dad smirked.

"Doesn't mean it's Bigfoot," Rick said, his tone more petulant than he intended. "Probably means a deer died and its carcass is rotting somewhere over there."

His father shook his head, a disappointed expression darkening his face.

"Come on," Rick said, "you don't really believe there's a big, hairy man-thing skulking behind that pine tree, do you?"

"You've seen the footprints yourself, on previous expeditions."

Yes, Rick had been on so many of these blasted Bigfoot hunts that he'd seen just about everything the woods could offer. Deer poop. Bear poop. The footprints of a barefoot human. ATV tire tracks. Half-eaten apples. Garbage left behind by people who themselves qualified as garbage. Never had he seen a Bigfoot, but a few times Dad pointed out to him faint impressions in the soil and pronounced the marks "forest ape tracks." Thanks to his father's Bigfoot history lessons, Rick knew historically the mythical beasts had been known as wild men, though his father rarely used the term. At first Dad called the mythical monsters Bigfoot, then Sasquatch, and lately forest apes. What next, hirsute brethren of the earth?

Rick sighed. "Those depressions could've been anything. Bear tracks, erosion, the mark left by somebody's behind..."

"You saw the toe impressions."

"I saw what you called toe impressions. Didn't look like much to me."

His father shook his head again, frowning.

"Tell me this," Rick said. "If Bigfoot's real, why hasn't anybody found a dead one, or the bones of one?"

"When was the last time you saw a dead bear? Or any other dead animal? Carcasses are recycled by the scavengers and the environment."

Rick said nothing. His father had a point. Despite spending countless hours in the woods, he'd rarely seen any dead animal, and never a dead bear. Still, the evidence that convinced his father failed to convince him. Stories told by people who claimed to see something. Impressions in the dirt. Nasty smells. None of it seemed concrete to Rick. Besides, nothing as bizarre as Bigfoot could possibly exist. Where would it fit into the evolutionary scheme of things?

Dad was staring at him without expression. Rick knew that meant his father was insulted.

"I'm sorry," Rick said. "I wish I could believe like you do. But I don't."

A breeze blew over them. The stench intensified, so strong now that Rick resorted to breathing through his mouth. His father walked toward the pine tree. Rick trailed behind him.

Ee-yoop.

Dad froze, and Rick bumped into him before he too halted. The cry came from beyond the pine tree. The stench was overpowering now, eliciting a gag response in Rick's throat. He swallowed hard against the gorge and raised a hand to cover his nose and mouth. His father craned his neck to squint at the pine tree, which stood thirty feet away.

Grrrrrr.

Goosebumps popped out up and down Rick's arms. The growling came from behind the pine tree, he thought, but closer than the whoop had sounded.

He tugged his father's sleeve, whispering, "Let's go, Dad. Whatever wild animal that is, I think we ticked it off."

"If so, then running is also a bad idea. Could trigger the creature's hunting instinct."

A chill shimmied down Rick's spine. Hunting instinct. Great. They probably had an irate wolf or bear stalking them, and if they ran, the beast might attack them.

Creature. His father had called the animal a creature, the word he sometimes used in lieu of his other names for Bigfoot.

Rick scowled at his father. "You still think it's Bigfoot."

His father was silent.

"Gimme a break, it's probably a bear."

Dad raised a hand to silence him. Rick stared past the pine tree to the area on which his father's gaze remained locked. He saw nothing.

"Oogah."

Rick glanced at his father. "Did you say something?"

Dad mouthed "no" as he pointed a finger at the pine tree.

"You think the tree spoke?"

His father flashed an irritated look at him. Rick mentally slapped himself. Of course his father didn't think the tree spoke. Charles

Bergren might be a little flaky, but he held onto enough of his wits to know trees didn't speak.

But the grunted syllables had almost sounded like words.

Ee-yoop.

The cry pierced the air, loud and sharp as a bullhorn. Rick winced. From the right, farther away, another cry echoed through the forest. Even further away, several whoops answered the first two, the cries overlapping each other.

Crunch, crunch, crunch.

The sound faded into the distance. Rick stood motionless, his voice mute, the goosebumps on his arms refusing to go away. The crunching had sounded like footsteps. But footsteps of what?

His father blew out a breath. Rick glanced at him. Dad started for the pine tree, motioning for Rick to follow. In a minute they reached the tree, and his father stooped to examine the ground. Dad rose and walked circles around the tree, widening the circle with every revolution. His gaze stayed fixed on the ground, his jaw set, his lips flattened into a line.

Rick listened, but he heard no more whoops. No footsteps either, other than Dad's.

After several minutes, his father stopped. He kneeled and lowered one hand almost to the ground, hovering it a few inches from the dirt. With his free hand, motioned for Rick to approach.

Rick squatted beside his father.

"Look at this," Dad said as he traced a shape in the air with his index finger.

Leaning over, Rick squinted at the depression his father had indicated. It looked vaguely foot shaped, with five smaller impressions at one end, similar to toes in a human footprint. The whole print looked sort of...blurry. The soft soil retained the impression of whatever had touched it, but the details were lost.

"I suppose you think this is a Bigfoot track," Rick said.

"Yes."

"Come on, Dad, it could be anything."

His father rose, stretched. "Well, it's not good enough to cast or photograph. But it is evidence that something large walked through here."

A snide retort popped into Rick's brain. He bit it back.

His father sighed. "I suspect one day you'll be forced to open your eyes and your mind to the full spectrum of possibilities the universe offers." Dad straightened his backpack and, as he walked away, said over his shoulder, "You'll be a lot more fun to talk to then."

Rick lingered there for a moment, studying the blurry imprint in the soil.

A chill tingled on his neck. He swiveled his head to look behind. Nothing there, naturally.

"Let's go, Rick."

Standing up, he turned to trudge after his father.

"Oogah."

The grunted word came from behind. The sound was quiet, barely a whisper.

In slow motion, Rick pivoted his head. A breeze wafted a sickening smell over him.

Could it be?

No. He grasped the straps of his backpack and marched toward his father. It wasn't. He probably imagined the sound and the smell, his mind spurred on by his father's pronouncements that huge, hairy man-beasts roamed these woods. Whatever had been watching him, it was most definitely not a Bigfoot.

The goosebumps on his arms disagreed.

The hell with goosebumps. It was not Bigfoot.

As he stomped after his father, he did not look back.

The Cost

SOMETHING BEAUTIFUL HAPPENED TO A PERSON IN the woods. Most folks ignored it. But for those who paid attention—left their cell phones in the car, abandoned their MP3 players and laptop computers—the woods bestowed on them a magical gift.

Silence.

Not complete silence, of course. It was, however, the kind of silence that residents of metropolitan areas never knew unless they ventured beyond the city limits.

Charlie Bergren knew the silence. He counted it among his best friends. Most people might call him crazy for thinking of silence as a steadfast and true friend. But no one who had ever entered the woods and let themselves get immersed in it would see anything odd about his relationship with the silence.

Well, maybe they would. He just didn't care either way.

If he didn't mind his own son thinking he was nuts, then why on earth should he care what strangers thought about him?

Standing there in the midst of the forest, eyes closed and ears open, Charlie let the silence wash over him and seep into his pores. The woods did at first seem quiet. No honking car horns. No blaring radios with bass beats that triggered small earthquakes. No sirens. No people chattering. No mechanical noises of any kind. Just the whispering of his own breaths.

And the heartbeat of nature.

The woods were alive. Its breaths rattled the leaves, creating a sound not unlike the whispering of his own breathing. Game trails served as the arteries transporting life throughout the body of the woods. If a person relaxed and really listened, he would hear the woods speaking to him. Chickadees, finches, and sparrows twittered away in the treetops. In the distance a raven squawked once, and then twice. Somewhere deeper in the woods, a tree creaked in a sudden gust of wind.

Bleep. Bleep-bleep.

The distinctly electronic sound snapped Charlie out of his reverie. He opened his eyes and looked to his right.

The pretty young woman standing six feet away held a cell phone in one hand while with the other hand she punched buttons on its keypad. The breeze tousled her chestnut hair. She reached up to bat the locks away from her face.

"What are you doing?" Charlie asked.

She looked up, focusing her green eyes on him. "Huh?"

"I asked," Charlie said, "what you're doing with that phone. We're supposed to be hunting, Katy."

Rolling her eyes, she responded, "I just wanted to see if there's a signal out here. There isn't."

"We're in the woods. Relax your death grip on technology."

She sighed, then stuffed the phone in her jacket pocket.

Charlie shook his head. Although he knew Katy loved the woods is much as he did, she harbored a lingering attachment to the technology of the modern world. He liked technology too. His TV and satellite dish provided entertainment when he was too tired to read. His cell phone had saved his butt when his car broke down on a lonely stretch of road. His computer improved his work efficiency and let him explore a world of possibilities on the Internet. Yet all of technology's strengths did not blind him to its weaknesses.

Surfing the Internet could never take the place of immersing oneself in the woods. E-mail and cell phones could never replace human contact.

Adjusting the straps of her backpack, Katy asked, "So how does a hunt like this work?"

Charlie shrugged.

Katy locked those green eyes on his face. She pursed her lips.

He aimed a tight smile at her. She probably took it as sarcasm, but his expression actually arose from a completely different source. He had no idea how a hunt like this worked. Maybe no one did. He knew even less about the subject than some other people might. Folks who engaged in this type of hunting seemed to make it up as they went along, so why shouldn't he?

Hunting had never been his strong suit. Killing animals for sport appealed to him about as much as diving with sharks. Well, maybe hunting appealed to him a bit more than that. At least in deer hunting the prey seemed unlikely to disembowel the hunter. Of course, referring to the current endeavor as hunting seemed misleading, if not completely erroneous. Nothing would die today.

Unless he made a horrible mistake.

Katy planted her hands on her hips. "I thought you did this kind of thing all the time. But you act like you don't have a clue what you're doing."

"I don't." He was secure enough to admit it, though Katy seemed unimpressed with his honesty. When she scrunched up her entire face into an expression of frustrated confusion, he said, "I have done this before. But I've never had much of a clue what I'm doing. I learn as I go."

"How successful have you been?"

"Moderately."

Truthfully, he'd found limited success in the field. Most of his successes unfolded out of sheer luck. He stumbled into the right set of circumstances while following leads provided by individuals he considered reliable. As reliable as any eyewitness could be.

Katy dropped her hands to her sides. Her expression wilted. She muttered something he couldn't quite hear, then said, "We've been out here for over an hour. If neither of us knows what the hell we're doing, how on earth are we supposed to hunt for Bigfoot?"

Good question, he thought, but said, "Common sense and intuition."

"I've been told I don't have any common sense."

"Don't believe everything you're told."

He started down the trail again. Tall weeds scraped against the fabric of his jeans. If he picked up ticks today, he supposed that would serve him right. His colleagues thought he was senile, and maybe they were right. Only a senile old man would drag a young woman into the woods to hunt for a creature the scientific establishment said did not and could not exist. Not for the first time today, he wondered why Katy was here.

She answered his classified ad. That was the simple answer. The genuine, deeper answer eluded him. What kind of woman answered an ad seeking an assistant to work in, as he phrased it in the ad, a ridiculed field of research? The ad also mentioned the work involved huge hairy creatures and inclement weather. He figured anyone who responded to such an ad would bring the right combination of curiosity, humor, and resistance to mockery. Katy certainly brought those qualities. He'd also expected that anyone who answered the ad might be a little off-kilter, which he could handle—provided they weren't flaky as a French pastry. Katy proved neither flaky nor off-kilter. She had her quirks, for sure, but in the few weeks he'd known her, he'd grown fond of her in a fatherly way.

Which reminded him of something.

"You're still coming over for dinner tomorrow night," he asked, "aren't you?"

"Uh-huh," Katy said, her attention on the woods around them.

"Wear something nice."

She jerked her head to look at him. Crinkling her brow, she asked, "Why?"

Yes, she was suspicious. Always. Not to the point of paranoia, though.

"It's a special occasion," he said. "We're celebrating the grand opening of the Human Origins Project."

"Oh." The suspicious crinkle ironed out of her brow. "I still don't get why you call your group that. It's about Bigfoot hunting, right? The Bigfoot Research Project would seem more appropriate."

"I suspect the origins of Bigfoot and humans are intertwined in some way. And I prefer to call them hairy hominids."

"Right. I keep forgetting."

Katy returned her attention to the woods and they continued down the trail. Charlie felt a little guilty about misleading her. Tomorrow night's dinner party included a surprise that she may or may not like. He hoped she would like it. But the surprise involved a volatile element beyond his control. Not that he expected violence. The volatile element was intellectual rather than physical. He intended to introduce Katy to another potential member of their project. Though he hoped Katy and the potential member would hit it off, Charlie recognized the possibility that she just might go ballistic when she discovered the surprise.

There might be violence after all.

Plop.

An apple hit the ground several feet in front of him. Charlie halted, mesmerized by the small red fruit.

"What was that?" Katy asked.

She came up behind him to peer around his shoulder at the object lying in the trail.

Holding the rest of his body still, Charlie rotated his head to survey the area around them. Evergreens and hardwoods dominated the forest. He saw no apple trees.

The apple had sailed down from above.

Charlie tilted his head back to study the higher boughs of the trees. No apples up there.

"Are you superstitious about walking past an apple?" Katy said. "Is it like a black cat crossing your path?"

The sarcasm in her tone did not escape him. He decided to ignore it, however, because it felt more like affectionate teasing than true ridicule. So he said, "It apparently fell out of the clear blue sky."

"It's raining apples?"

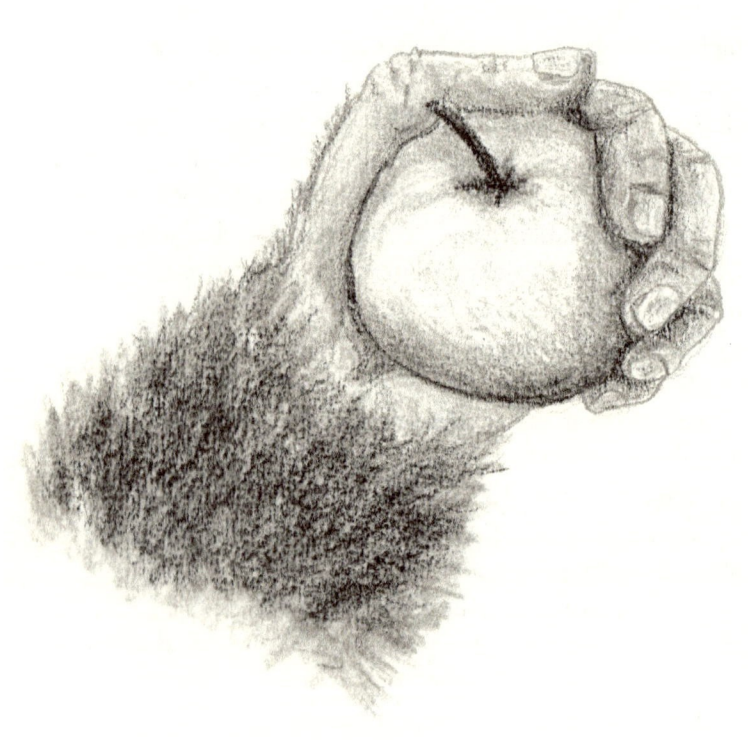

"Maybe." He twisted his head around to look at her. "Then again, witnesses have reported having rocks thrown at them by hairy hominids. Why not apples?"

Katy stepped around him to kneel by the apple. She picked up the fruit and turned it in her hand as if scrutinizing its surface. After a moment, she set down the apple.

"I've had rocks thrown at me," she said, without rising or looking up at him. "I can't say for sure it was Bigf—a hairy hominid. But I had my suspicions."

"When did this happen?"

"Back in college. In California."

He waited for her to say more. When a minute or two passed without a word uttered or an apple thrown, he said, "Why don't we press on? Maybe our woodland grocer will show his face if we act like we don't care."

She cast a skeptical look in his direction.

He tromped past her. She hesitated for a second, but then started after him.

Minutes elapsed. The tree cover thickened until the boughs overhead formed a canopy that shaded them from the sun. Here and there, blades of light sliced down through the foliage.

The sound of Katy's footfalls behind him ceased.

Charlie glanced over his shoulder. Katy had stopped to stare into the woods to their right. She tilted her head in that direction, opening her mouth a little. The technique was supposed to make it easier to hear faint sounds. He hadn't taught her that. She told him about it.

"What is it?" Charlie whispered.

"Not sure." Katy squinted into the woods. "I heard something moving around."

He tracked the line of her gaze through the gap between two large trees, into an area populated by saplings and bathed in darkly golden light. Nothing popped out at him. Whatever she'd heard, either the sound stopped or his hearing wasn't as sharp as hers. He heard nothing.

A sapling shimmied.

"There," Katy said, jabbing a finger in the air to point toward the sapling. "Did you see that? Something is definitely back there."

"Could be a deer or bear."

"Or a hairy hominid."

Another sapling swayed.

Katy bolted toward the saplings.

"Wait!" Charlie shouted, but Katy ignored him.

He took three steps to follow her. She'd taken off so fast that she disappeared from view within seconds, her silhouette engulfed by the foliage.

A cry punctured the silence.

Charlie froze. The cry was not a scream. It sounded more like a wordless, disgusted exclamation. He ran toward the area where the cry had originated. As he ducked around one of the larger trees, he caught sight of Katy several yards ahead of him. Her back was to him. She stood motionless, shoulders hunched, head bowed, hands fisted at her sides.

Skidding to a halt, he eyed her from the backside.

"Katy?" he said. "Are you hurt?"

"No," she snapped.

Just then the stench reached his nostrils. Skunk.

Katy slowly turned around to face him. She scuffled toward him. As she approached within ten feet of him, he realized the stench emanated from her. The flush that burned on her cheeks probably stemmed from a mixture of anger and humiliation, the two emotions that darkened her expression. He switched to breathing through his mouth, which helped some.

"You got sprayed," he said.

"Yes," she replied, the final consonant hissing from her lips. "Bigfoot hunting sucks."

"Hairy hominids are reputed to smell bad," he said. "Bigfoot hunters aren't supposed to, though."

"Thank you."

He reached out to pat her shoulder empathetically, but the god-awful smell stopped him. He settled for giving her what he hoped came out as an empathetic look. She really did stink horribly, and he really did feel for her. Although he never had the misfortune of getting sprayed by a skunk, he knew several dogs who had.

Katy let out a sharp sigh. "I think I've had my fill of Bigfoot hunting for today."

"I can imagine." He gestured for her to follow him as he headed back toward the trail. "Let's get you home so you can take a nice hot shower and change into clean clothes. You'll feel better then."

"I need an acid shower."

"The smell's not that bad."

Despite his words, he continued to breathe through his mouth as they hustled back down the trail toward the gravel road they'd parked on before embarking on their hairy hominid hunt. This was state land, but he preferred to enter the woods from less-traveled paths. By the time they arrived at Charlie's pickup truck, Katy had relaxed somewhat. Her hands were no longer balled into tight fists and the flush had left her cheeks.

She still looked disgusted, however.

Once they both climbed inside the truck, Charlie started the engine and rolled down the windows. Air conditioning would not suffice today. They needed a massive influx of fresh air.

Katy glanced at him sideways, her eyes narrowed. "I thought the smell wasn't that bad."

"It isn't, uh..." He struggled for a white lie she might believe. "I think there's a dead mouse in the engine compartment. The rancid odor was bothering me on the drive out here."

"Cut the crap, Charlie," Katy said. "I stink worse than a dead body that's been lying in a mud puddle for three days."

This time he pushed through the revulsion to clap a hand on her shoulder. As he squeezed lightly, he said, "Yes, you do. But all things pass in time. And don't worry, I won't tell a soul what happened today."

She made a face that either signified resignation or meant she was plotting his death by the most painful means imaginable.

He decided to believe the former.

"Thanks for the platitude," Katy muttered.

He withdrew his hand, shifted the truck into drive, and executed a U-turn. They drove down the road in silence for five minutes, maybe longer.

Finally, Katy said, "I thought it was a Bigfoot."

"What?"

"The skunk. I thought...the trees shaking, it made me think a big animal was hiding back there."

Charlie sighed. "Next time, exercise a bit more caution before racing headlong into the unknown."

She leaned her head back against the headrest. When he glanced at her, he saw that her eyes were closed. Her head lolled to the left. Just when he decided she'd fallen asleep, Katy spoke.

"I've wanted to see a Bigfoot for so long," she told him, "that I really wanted this to be my chance. Why do other people get to see one, and not me? People who have no interest in Bigfoot, who think it's all a hoax, they get to see one. It's not fair."

"I know," he said. "But life isn't—"

She swung her head up. "If you feed me another platitude, I swear I'll vomit."

"Sorry."

Katy groaned. "The stink is not letting up. You might not want me to come over for dinner tomorrow."

"Oh, the stink will be gone by then." He steered the truck around a curve, then said, "This is the cost of believing in Bigfoot, Katy. Everyone thinks you're nuts and the evidence you desperately want to collect never pans out."

She said nothing as she turned her head to gaze out the passenger window.

He knew the cost of believing all too well. Sometimes he cursed the hairy hominids for tantalizing him with ambiguous sightings and morsels of physical evidence. The morsels never satiated his hunger for proof or knowledge. He'd settle for understanding what the hairy hominids were and where they came from. Yet he accepted that he might never know.

Keeping his gaze on the road, he asked, "Are you quitting the Human Origins Project?"

She didn't answer for a moment. He opened his mouth to repeat the question, thinking she hadn't heard him.

"No," Katy said at last. "I'll stick it out. Can't let the debunkers win."

He smiled. "Nope, we can't have that."

As long as people kept believing and kept searching, the debunkers would never win.

He glanced out the window at the woods. Sooner or later, he would find the proof he hungered for—though perhaps that proof would never garner scientific acceptance. Knowing for himself would be enough.

Katy cleared her throat.

He looked at her. Eyes closed, she leaned her head against the door so that the clean air blowing through the window buffeted her face. Curly locks of her hair bounced in the wind.

Then again, maybe he wouldn't be the one to find the proof. Maybe someone else would. Maybe that someone was Katy.

The truck jounced over a pothole. Returning his attention to the road, Charlie mentally chewed on the notion that had just occurred to him. Who would complete the hunt for Bigfoot? One day, he'd find out.

And the outcome might prove worth the cost of believing.

The Bigfoot Effect

THE WOODS LOOKED HARMLESS ENOUGH, BUT HIS FATHER was a different matter.

Rick stood at a fork in the trail, in more senses than one. First, he stood at an actual fork in the game trail they had been following for the past ten minutes. Second, he stood at a metaphorical fork in the trail of his relationship with his father. He knew this, but he didn't know what to do about it.

A frown tightened his features. Despite his college degree, he never felt intellectual or even smarter than average. Becoming an accountant didn't exactly mark him as an intellectual heavyweight. He wasn't inclined toward self-reflection—in fact, he tried to avoid it—and he certainly wasn't prone to deep thinking. Not that he was stupid or shallow. He just didn't see the point.

So now Rick found himself at the fork in the trail with his father alongside him. Neither had said anything since they climbed out of the pickup truck and started down the trail. During the twenty-minute drive from his father's house, they did nothing but bicker. Rick hated arguing with his father. He hated arguing, period. Sometimes, though, he just couldn't stop himself from contradicting Dad. The elder Bergren seemed to relish making ridiculous statements that diverged on the utterly insane, just to see the reaction he would get from his son. Rick tried to restrain himself. It rarely worked.

Maybe if he'd indulged in a little navel-gazing he'd know how to deal with his father.

Dad raised both arms, indicating each trail with the corresponding arm as he said, "Which shall it be? Right or left?"

Rick shrugged.

His father turned sideways to look at him. "Come on, take a risk. There's no one here to ridicule you for choosing a trail."

"Tell me again why we're here."

"Because there have been half a dozen sightings in this area during the past month."

"Sightings of..."

"Hairy hominids."

Rick snorted. "Bigfoot. And so we're here to..."

"See what we can see."

"Wonderful," Rick said, unable to quash the derisive tone in his voice.

"Besides, you said you missed the woods after spending eight hours a day inside a windowless cubicle." Dad shrugged. "At least you're in the woods now."

"With Bigfoot, according to you."

He knew his father disliked the term Bigfoot and vacillated between alternative terms, but lately Dad preferred hairy hominids, as if that term sounded better or more believable than Bigfoot. No matter what anyone called it, Bigfoot was nothing more than a hoax or a myth. His father believed in it anyway, insisting that one day Rick would believe in it too.

Like hell. He'd believe in Bigfoot when one of two things happened—either the sun turned into a smiley face or a Bigfoot threw him over its shoulder and dragged him off to its cave.

"Why do you insist," Dad said, "on asking me the same questions over and over?"

"I guess for the same reason that you keep trying to brainwash me into believing in Bigfoot."

"I'm not asking you to believe in anything. I hate to see you go through life so closed minded and dogmatic about what is or is not possible, that's all."

"And I hate to see my father join the lunatic fringe." Rick felt his frown deepening into a scowl and tried to shake it off. Sighing, he said, "I come to visit for a few days and I wind up taking part in a Bigfoot hunt. I can't believe I agreed to this."

Dad chuckled. "Neither can I."

"What?" Rick glanced sideways at his father. "Why did you ask me to come along if you didn't think I would?"

"I'm an eternal optimist."

Rick had to agree with that assessment. Only a diehard optimist would take up Bigfoot hunting as a hobby. For a few years now, his father had actively collected via telephone and e-mail supposed sightings of ape-men in Michigan. He used classified ads to promote his endeavors, and eventually his eccentric pastime became common knowledge among the locals. Every time some yahoo called or e-mailed in a sighting report, Charles Bergren abandoned his duties as a college professor to rush out to the scene of the purported incident. Sometimes he found impressions in the ground that he identified as Bigfoot tracks. Most of the time, he seemed to find nothing.

At least nothing he told Rick about.

Dad faced the fork in the trail. "Well, what'll it be?"

The path was not a formal trail used by hikers and other tourists. Wildlife made these trails, which were narrow and somewhat over-grown. Dad insisted that if they wanted to see Bigfoot, they must enter the woods on a game trail rather than a prepared pathway.

Rick looked at the right-hand trail, then the one on the left. Which way did Bigfoot lie? Neither, he knew. But his father wanted him to choose, and when Dad wanted something he kept pestering until he got it.

"Tell you what," Rick said, "why don't you take the right one and I'll take the left one? That'll give us the best chance of catching a...hairy whatsit."

"Hairy hominid." Dad hesitated. "I'm not sure we should split up."

"We've got these," Rick said, patting the two-way radio clipped onto his belt.

Now it was his father's turn to frown. "I know. But you aren't as experienced in the woods. I'd feel better if we stayed together."

"I'm not a complete idiot. I can handle myself just fine without you to hold my hand."

His father stared straight ahead at the large pine tree that squatted between the two trails. Although the tree must've risen twenty feet in the air, its bulk stemmed not from height but rather from the width of its body that split into multiple trunks. It looked like a giant broccoli.

"We should split up," Rick said. "Unless you don't really want to find Bigfoot."

That did the trick.

Letting out an annoyed sigh, his father said, "Fine, we'll try it your way."

Rick suppressed the smirk he felt tugging at his lips. Finally, he discovered the secret to getting *his* way with his father. Use Bigfoot as leverage.

Shrugging the backpack off his shoulders, Dad unzipped one of the pack's compartments and brought out a revolver. The gun sat snug inside a belt holster.

Dad offered Rick the holster and gun. "At least take this."

His father carried a rifle over one shoulder. Rick knew Dad brought the handgun as backup, though backup for what kind of situation, he couldn't say. Maybe he didn't want to know.

"You do remember how to use a gun," his father said, "don't you?"

"Of course I do."

Rick snatched the holster from his father's grasp. Then he realized that's exactly what his father had wanted him to do, and he groaned. He supposed it was too much to hope that he might outwit his father more than once in one day.

Or in one month.

After attaching the holster to his belt, which required removing the belt first, Rick patted the holstered weapon. He flashed his father an are-you-happy-now look.

Dad nodded. "I'll take the right-hand trail."

He marched off down the trail.

"What should I do?" Rick called after his father.

"Take the other trail and keep your eyes peeled for evidence." Dad paused to glance over his shoulder at Rick. "And try not to be such a debunker about it."

With that, his father sauntered off into the woods. In half a minute or so, the shadows of the forest swallowed him.

Rick moseyed down the left-hand trail. Other than the occasional pile of deer scat, aka poop, he saw nothing of interest. Not that he found deer poop interesting. But at least the scat reminded him that actual animals left actual evidence of their actual presence in the woods. Imaginary creatures, on the other hand, left only inconclusive evidence that remained open to interpretations unbounded by reason or the rules of scientific evidence.

His father was a history professor, not a biologist. Why should anyone accept his ambiguous evidence?

Rick grimaced. A son ought to believe his own father, he supposed. He felt like a jerk of the first order for treating his father like a wacko. Dad was passionate about everything he believed in, from his take on historical events to his research into the Bigfoot phenomenon. Rick envied his father's passion and dedication. His own job inspired neither. Crunching numbers all day let him earn a living, but it fell short of giving him purpose. Such a huge abyss yawned between him and purpose that he couldn't even see the other side.

Still, he didn't begrudge his father the right to find purpose and happiness in life. He just wished his dad would choose a less-embarrassing hobby.

Why couldn't his father find passion and purpose in trout fishing?

The trail wound through the woods, skirting downed trees. Rick hiked onward without a clue what he was supposed to be doing. He really should've asked Dad for some detailed instructions before taking off on his own. Bigfoot hunting seemed to involve looking for vague evidence, which made it difficult for him to know when he spotted anything his father might deem significant.

He couldn't find imaginary proof. At best, he might find signs of activity that seemed out of the ordinary. Sure, that cleared things up perfectly. Look for signs of unusual activity. No problem.

Try not to be such a debunker about it.

His father's words returned to him now. They constituted the sole instruction the elder Bergren gave to his son. Although Rick wondered what the words meant at the time, his father took off into the woods without giving him a chance to ask for clarification. Dad bemoaned debunkers even more than politicians, and he despised politicians. Debunkers worked from the assumption, Dad said, that Bigfoot was a hoax or a delusion and that all evidence gathered concerning the creature resulted from those two sources. Footprints were hoaxed. Witnesses were deluded. According to his father, debunkers never bothered to actually examine the evidence before denouncing it as baloney.

When Dad told him not to be a debunker about it, he must've meant that Rick should remove his skeptical blinders. Look for anything out of place. Anything that didn't belong. Signs not readily attributable to known wildlife or human activity.

Okay. He supposed he could do that. If for no other reason than to make his father happy, he would try not to scoff at every little thing. He knew he scoffed at everything his father said about Bigfoot. He didn't mean to, really. The words popped out of his mouth as if a spirit possessed him. Except he didn't believe in ghosts either.

A shape on the ground captured his attention, and he knelt to examine it. The impression was shallow, but still deeper than his own boot prints, which left only the slightest marks. The impression measured much longer and wider than his own tracks. Unlike his boot prints, though, the impression lacked the criss-crossing lines of a boot sole. It also lacked the arch of a bare footprint.

The impression angled across the narrow trail, as if whatever left it had crossed over the trail rather than walking down it.

Rick stepped off the trail. Walking lightly alongside the trail, he continued onward while scanning the ground for more impressions. About forty feet down the trail, he spotted one. Then another. And another. No more than four feet separated each impression. The trackway led him straight down the trail to another fork in the path. This time, the trail seemed to split for no particular reason.

A breeze rustled the leaves above his head. He tilted his head back to watch the foliage swaying gently. He really did miss the woods.

A scuffling sound issued from his left.

Rick jerked his head in that direction. He squinted into the woods.

Nothing. Trees, trees, and more trees. Weeds and bushes filled in the gaps. He'd probably heard a rabbit or a grouse moving around in the brush.

He took a step and then froze as movement flashed to his left.

Too big for a grouse or rabbit. Too tall for a deer. Nothing could stand that tall except a man, or maybe a black bear raised on its hind legs. Why a bear might walk in an upright stance, he couldn't figure.

The tracks. The humanlike-yet-not-human footprints he'd followed down the trail.

What might leave tracks like that?

A bear? No. What else?

Resting his hand on the revolver's grip, he turned toward the left.

The tall shape ducked behind a pine tree.

Rick tore through the brush, heading straight for the pine tree. The figure darted out from behind the tree and took off in the opposite direction. Rick hurtled after the whatever-it-was, his long legs carrying him faster than the shorter figure ahead of him. Since Rick stood over six feet tall, his quarry might not be short but simply shorter than he was. He couldn't get a good look at the figure as they stampeded through the woods. Man, beast...who knew?

Not a bear, that was for sure.

The figure tripped, tumbling forward.

Rick skidded to a halt a few feet away. His breaths came in hard gasps.

The figure lay prone on the ground, surrounded by weeds, groaning softly.

It was a person. Dressed in camouflage. Dark hair sticking out from under a knit cap. A backpack slung over one shoulder.

The person rolled over. The backpack slid off into the weeds. It was a man, Rick saw now. Though dirt smudged the guy's face, he looked otherwise unharmed.

As his breathing normalized, Rick scowled at the man. He said, "Are you stalking me?"

The man stared at him without blinking for several seconds. Then the guy said, in a tentative voice, "Uh-uh."

"Then what the hell were you doing?"

Pushing up into a sitting position, the man said, "Nothing."

Rick grabbed the man's arm and hauled him onto his feet.

The backpack caught Rick's eye. The main compartment was partially unzipped. A piece of wood jutted out. A piece of wood with a familiar shape and dirt clinging to its underside. He could just make out a second, similar piece of wood inside the pack.

Rick snatched up the backpack, ripped open the zipper, and yanked out the pieces of wood.

"Hey!" the man shouted, grabbing for the wood slabs.

"What is this?" Rick asked.

He took one of the pieces of wood in each hand and turned them side to side to examine their surfaces. They were shaped like the impressions he'd seen in the soil on the trail.

Shaking his head, Rick tossed the wooden footprints at the man. The guy caught one, but the other clattered to the ground.

"You're out here faking Bigfoot tracks," Rick said. "Haven't you got anything better to do? Like, I don't know, toilet-papering houses?"

The guy looked a little old for teenage pranks. He must have the emotional maturity of a fifteen-year-old boy, though, considering that he was out here hoaxing Bigfoot tracks. If Dad were here, he'd give the guy a serious dressing-down.

"It's just for kicks," the guy whined. "Everybody's talking about the old guy who's been looking for Sasquatch out here. He's totally senile."

Rick seized the front of the man's shirt and shook him. The twerp's eyes bulged and he dropped the wooden footprint. It landed on the ground atop the other one, striking it with a clack.

"That old guy," Rick said through clenched teeth, "is my father."

The man's face blanched. "S-sorry, dude, I didn't know. I'm sure he's totally cool."

Rick let go of the man. He managed to separate his jaws long enough to say, "Get out of here." He kicked the wooden footprints. "And take your asinine hobby with you."

The man slung the backpack over one shoulder and grabbed his wooden footprints, hugging them to his chest. He stammered another apology, then scurried back in the direction from which they'd both come.

Rick strode back toward the trail too. He had no trouble finding his way back, what with the damage both he and the hoaxer had inflicted on the foliage. He just followed the trail of destruction.

A few minutes later, he stepped out onto the trail again. He stopped there and took a moment to consider his options. Once he reached a decision, he plucked the two-way radio from his belt and pressed the talk button.

"You there, Dad?" he said into the radio.

A second later, his father's voice crackled back to him. "I hear you. Something wrong?"

"No." Rick hesitated, then said, "I think I solved your Bigfoot mystery. Meet me back at the fork in the trail where we split up."

"Okey-doke."

He'd expected his father to argue, at least a little bit. A sliver of unease lodged in Rick's mind. Charles Bergren said nothing when his son claimed to have solved the Bigfoot mystery after spending ten minutes in the wilderness. The crafty codger must have something up his sleeve.

Heading back down the trail toward the designated meeting place, Rick passed by the trackway created by the hoaxer. He paused to kneel beside one of the tracks. It had sharp edges. Not surprising given that slabs of carved wood, rather than genuine feet, left the impressions.

He continued down the trail. The trackway ended and, forty feet later, he came upon the single track that angled across the trail. It was the first impression he'd noticed during his trek. Crouching, he studied the impression for the second time.

Superficially, it looked like the tracks seen further down the trail. The tracks created by the hoaxer. When he really studied them, however, differences emerged. The hoaxed tracks had sharp edges, but this one did not. The hoaxed tracks also did not impress into the ground half as deep as this track. Though he hardly qualified as an expert in footprints, of any kind, even he recognized that this track must've come from a different source than the hoaxed trackway found further down the trail.

What made this track?

He struggled to squelch the one word that wanted to pop into his mind. It wasn't. It couldn't be.

Was it?

No. The track had not been left by a Bigfoot.

He could almost convince himself to dismiss it. A feather of doubt tickled his subconscious, but he'd gotten pretty good at ignoring such instincts. His father would call it denial. He called it common sense.

At least, he hoped it was common sense.

What would his father do? Follow the line of travel indicated by the track and search for other prints in the vicinity.

Rick tried to motivate himself to do that. Really, he tried. The urge to leave the area and forget about it was too strong.

So he left the area. Forgetting about it, that wasn't so easy.

Shortly, he found himself at the fork in the trail where he and his father had gone their separate ways. Dad stood precisely at the split in the path, his expression serene, one hand grasping the strap of his backpack where it crossed in front of his shoulder.

"Okay," his father said, "let's hear it."

Rick stopped a few feet from his father. "Hear what?"

"Your solution to the Bigfoot mystery."

Rick pretended to adjust the straps of his backpack. He gazed past his father's shoulder into the trees, because he couldn't look the older man in the eye as he said, "I found a hoaxer making fake Bigfoot tracks."

"And how does that debunk the eyewitness sightings?"

"Uh, well...I guess the same guy or one of his buddies must've hoaxed the sightings too."

Dad walked up to him, clapped a hand on his shoulder, and said, "Now that's some convincing evidence you've got there, son."

Sighing, Rick twisted his lips into a warped frown. He thought back to the single footprint, different from the hoaxed trackway. He ought to tell his father about it. Yet he couldn't make the words come out of his mouth. They felt lodged in his throat. More likely, they were lodged in his subconscious right underneath a boulder of denial.

Dad shook his head. "Maybe you shouldn't come to dinner tonight."

"I thought you wanted to introduce me to the first member of your Bigfoot cult."

"Katy'll bite your head off and eat it for an appetizer."

Rick arched an eyebrow. "She sounds like a sweetheart."

His father chuckled. "She is—but she has an even lower tolerance for debunkers than I do."

As his father turned and started up the trail, Rick thought back on the way Dad described his new friend when convincing Rick to show up for dinner tonight. His father called the young woman "lovely, intelligent, and damn near fearless." He probably left out rude, loudmouthed, and totally insane. Anyone who responded to a classified ad seeking crackpots to join a Bigfoot group must need a few replacement screws installed in her brain.

He supposed he ought to meet her before calling the authorities to report he'd found their escaped mental patient. She might be nice. Maybe she was at least cute.

Besides, he just had to meet the girl who traipsed through the woods with his father on a quest to pin down the elusive Bigfoot. If Dad lavished high praise on her, then she must have something going for her. If he invited her on his woodland missions, then she must be special. Whether that meant special as in nuts or special as in extraordinary...

He'd find out tonight.

His father stopped to glance back at him. "You coming?"

"Yeah." Rick started after him. "Why aren't you upset I found a hoaxer out here? You hate those guys."

"Ah, but I have something they can never take away from me."

Rick stared at the back of his father's head as they marched down the trail. "What do you mean?"

"I had an experience of my own while you were chasing down hoaxers."

"Spit it out, Dad. What happened?"

His father glanced over his shoulder to smirk at Rick. He said, "I saw one."

"One what?"

"A creature."

Rick stopped dead.

After taking a few more steps, his father paused and turned around.

"I hope you're joking," Rick said.

"Nope." Dad smiled. "I was face-to-face with a hairy hominid not five minutes ago."

His father turned away and headed down the trail again.

Rick stood there for a moment, unable to speak or move. Thoughts bounced around in his brain until he felt dizzy from the mental commotion.

Could it be?

He swallowed against a lump in his throat. Had he found a genuine Bigfoot track?

No. That was nonsense. Bigfoot did not exist. He unmasked the hoaxer himself. The track he found separate from the others probably didn't look as different as he remembered. Memories played tricks sometimes, turning nothing into something.

Bigfoot absolutely, positively did not exist.

With his boulder of denial firmly in place again, he hurried down the trail after his father. He avoided thinking about the effect Bigfoot had on his life. He'd rather pretend the subject touched him only peripherally, in the form of his father's obsession. It didn't enter into his life directly. Certainly not today. Nothing happened to him in the woods. Nothing. And the other time, years ago, when he had a weird experience in the woods...

Nothing happened to him then either.

His father must've seen a bear just now.

They reached the truck and climbed inside. The drive home passed in silence. Rick didn't say a word about the single footprint.

And he never would.

A Hairy Situation

OW MUCH WOOD DID IT TAKE TO CONSTRUCT A FUNERAL
pyre?

Katy drummed the blunt end of her fork on the tabletop. The morbid thought about funeral pyres had popped into her mind unbidden, though not unprovoked. A multitude of snide comments coupled with snide facial expressions, all of it originating from a certain individual, triggered a string of bizarre and somewhat violent thoughts in her mind. A girl could only take so much. She found herself daydreaming about the various ways to both murder someone much larger than herself and to dispose of the dead body so that no one would find it.

She kept all of this to herself.

Across the table from her, the cause of her secret irritation gazed at her without expression now. Rick Bergren leaned back against his chair, one arm draped across the table alongside his dinner plate. Remnants of a meal littered the plate. He grabbed his almost-empty glass and swigged the remaining cola from it. After swallowing the liquid, he plunked the glass back onto the table and fixed his gaze on her once again.

Katy fidgeted in her seat. Though an overhead fixture provided most of the lighting, a candelabra positioned at the table's center cast flickering tongues of light through the room. The candlelight brought out the golden undertones in Rick's chocolate-colored hair, which was cut short. She looked into his eyes, with their irises as blue as gas flames, and tried to banish the irritation that simmered within her. Mostly, Rick seemed nice enough. But when a certain topic was raised, frequently by Rick himself, he couldn't conceal his disdain.

When Charlie invited her over for dinner at his new house, she assumed it would be the two of them. She, the new recruit into Charlie's Bigfoot investigation team, dining with her mentor. After all, Charlie's investigation team thus far consisted of just two people—Katy and Charlie. So she felt justified in her assumption that tonight's dinner would involve the two of them discussing the future of the investigation project. Instead, she arrived to find Charlie's son, Rick, setting the table with three place settings.

Every time Rick spoke the word Bigfoot, he sounded as if it physically hurt him to utter the syllables. Every time she tried to explain to Rick the evidence for Bigfoot's reality, he rolled his eyes at her. At those moments, she would glance around the room to assess the viability of various blunt objects that she might use as weapons to bludgeon Rick. The thought inevitably segued into an analysis of the possibilities for disposing of the body in such a way that Charlie wouldn't know she'd murdered his son. Not that she would ever do such a thing, but focusing on those thoughts kept her from yelling at Rick.

Rick arched an eyebrow at her. "Should I take your silence as a no?"

"Huh?"

"I asked if there's any actual, scientific evidence for the existence of Bigfoot."

Oh *that*. She'd forgotten he asked the question. Thoughts of corpse disposal distracted her to the point of mild amnesia.

"I already told you," she said, "there are eyewitness sightings and footprints and photographic evidence and hair samples and—"

"Right." Rick nodded, smirking. "And DNA testing said the hair came from...what was it again?"

"An unknown primate."

"Since people are primates, that isn't saying much."

"I know." The sharp tone in her voice dismayed her. Although she had to admit she harbored a temper, she rarely got this upset when confronted with dogmatic skepticism. What was wrong with her tonight? She took a deep breath, exhaled slowly, and then said, "That's why DNA evidence alone will never prove Bigfoot is real. But there's plenty of convincing circumstantial evidence that suggests these creatures do indeed exist."

"Nothing you've said so far has convinced me. I still say it's a load of cow manure."

This time she managed to sound calm as she said, "Have you examined any of the evidence yourself? Have you, I don't know, perhaps cracked open a single book on the subject before denouncing the evidence as cow manure?"

He shrugged. "I don't see the point."

She snorted. "I do. Your goal tonight seems to be to disabuse me of my beliefs using intimidation tactics and pitiful attempts to humiliate me." Laying both palms flat on the tabletop, she half rose from her chair and leaned over the table until less than two feet separated their faces. In a soft-yet-firm tone, she told him, "Let me tell you, buster, those tactics *never* work on me."

His jaw dropped open a smidge. His expression went blank, his eyes widening so subtly that she might not have noticed if she weren't leaning so close to him. Oh lord. She might've gone a little too far. It wasn't the first time. Going overboard was kind of a hobby for her.

Dropping back into her chair, she shut her eyes and sighed heavily.

She felt him staring at her. The sensation rippled down her spine as a chill.

Katy opened her eyes to find Rick watching her with an odd expression. Astonishment? Embarrassment? The look vanished before she could identify it, replaced by a neutral expression. He folded his hands on his lap. Averting his gaze, he pursed his lips.

They sat in silence for several seconds.

Then Rick looked up at her. "Dad told me you used to play the trumpet."

For a moment she stared at him, unable to comprehend his

statement. The change of topic had happened so abruptly that she got mental whiplash.

Okay, her outburst must've embarrassed him. In her experience, when confronted with things that disturbed them, men often reacted with anger. And it seemed that nothing disturbed a man quite as deeply as the notion of hairy, bipedal, nonhuman creatures haunting the woods. Hell, sometimes it disturbed her too.

"Yeah," she said, "I played the trumpet in school. I was a band geek."

"Me too." He smiled a little. "I played the flute."

She envisioned Rick, a strapping guy who stood over six feet tall, twittering away on a flute.

Laughter burst out of her. Too late, she clamped her mouth shut to restrain her guffaws. She really was making a fool of herself tonight. Oh well, she doubted she would ever see Rick Bergren again anyway, since he lived in Boston—and since he now realized she was utterly, irretrievably insane.

As her laughter at last subsided, she said, "Sorry. There weren't any male flutists in the bands I was in."

"Lots of pretty girls in the flute section, though."

She shook her head. "Men."

"If we'd gone to the same school, I would've taken up the trumpet."

A blush rose in her cheeks.

Time to change the subject. She asked, "Why are you so hostile to the idea of Bigfoot?"

"I'm not hostile." He hesitated. "Maybe I'm jaded about the subject because my father's been obsessed with Bigfoot since I was a teenager. He bought this house because somebody told him there were Bigfoot sightings in the area."

"I thought Charlie bought the house because he got it dirt cheap."

"That too."

Elsewhere in the house, a door banged shut. Katy glanced to her left, past the open kitchen, down the hallway toward the shadows that masked the door to the bathroom. Charlie strode out of the darkness, heading for the table. His gray hair and beard, both cropped short, gave him the look of a less-scruffy Santa.

Katy hopped up and intercepted Charlie before he reached the table. "May I have a word with you out on the deck please?"

"Certainly."

As she led him past the table toward the sliding glass doors, she avoided looking at Rick. The eerie feeling of being watched tingled down her spine again, and she couldn't help taking a quick sidelong peek at Rick. He was eyeing her with a strange expression, different from the odd look he'd gotten after her angry outburst. Katy focused on the sliding glass doors.

Once outside, she shut the door behind her and Charlie.

"Okay," she said, folding her arms over her chest, "would you care to tell me what the blazes you were thinking when you ambushed me with this little threesome tonight?"

"It's not an ambush." He feigned innocence, an act he pulled off better than anyone she knew. "Rick decided to fly in for a weekend visit, and I thought the two of you should meet."

She narrowed her eyes. "When did Rick inform you of his impending visit?"

He tapped a finger on his chin. "Hmm...it must've been Tuesday."

"The day before you invited me to dinner."

Now he feigned surprise. "Yes, I suppose it was. Huh."

"Don't *huh* me, Charlie. You knew exactly what you were doing, though I can't fathom what you were trying to accomplish by setting me up for a skeptic's ambush."

"That's not what I was setting you up for."

She scrunched her eyebrows. Although she thought she grasped his meaning, she refused to believe it. Charlie was a sneaky old coot, but still...

"Your son is rude," she told him. "And he's condescending."

Charlie started for the door.

She grabbed his arm. "Where do you think you're going?"

"To have a chat with Rick about his behavior this evening."

"Don't you dare."

He patted her hand. "Don't worry, I'll be discreet."

The mischievous gleam in his eyes awakened butterflies in her gut. He was up to something. Besides being a sneaky old coot, he was also nosy—at least when it came to her personal life. Yet he also had a talent for discretion. Whatever he intended to say to Rick, he would likely keep his true motivations hidden in the subtext.

Anyway, she could no more divert him from his current path, whatever it may be, than she could convince Rick that Bigfoot existed. Stubbornness seemed ingrained in the Bergren family DNA.

Katy released Charlie's arm. He moseyed back inside, sliding the door shut behind himself. Katy walked to the deck railing. Whatever Charlie was about to do, she did not want to witness it. Folding her arms atop the railing, she gazed out into the night. The light from inside the house petered out just past the deck. Hulking shapes taller than the house delineated the woods, though the darkness kept her from seeing much else. A creek wound its way past the house somewhere down below, as invisible as the woods.

Another chill rippled through her. She fought the urge to look over her shoulder for as long as she could, but after several seconds she gave up and turned her head.

Rick was watching her. Charlie sat across the table from him, in the chair Katy had vacated.

"Ee-yoop."

Katy jumped. The cry originated in the woods—close, from the sound of it. She squinted into the darkness, to no avail.

The sliding doors whooshed open. A tall shadow fell over the deck and railing beside her.

No sounds echoed from the woods. Not even a bug chirped.

Behind her, someone cleared his throat.

Katy turned to face Rick just as he reached the railing. Standing a couple feet away, he leaned one arm on the railing and angled his body toward her, those flame-blue eyes aimed straight into her gaze. A slight smile curved his lips.

She bit the inside of her lip. When Rick said nothing for twenty or thirty seconds, she asked, "What did you and Charlie talk about?"

Rick shrugged. "Bigfoot, naturally. Dad hardly talks about anything else these days."

Relief swept through Katy so quickly and powerfully that she felt woozy for a second.

"He told me about all the scientists and academics who've gotten involved in hunting for Bigfoot." Rick's smile turned rueful. "Apparently, I'm extremely closed minded about the subject. Dad says I need to broaden my perspective before he'll let me join your little club."

"But you don't want to join our club," she said. "Do you?"

"If I have to be a diehard believer to qualify for membership, then no."

"Belief is not a prerequisite. Being a diehard debunker, however, might disqualify you."

He opened his mouth as if to speak, then shut it again. Tapping a fingernail on the railing, he studied her with an unreadable expression.

She glanced out into the woods, into the deep and concealing darkness.

"You seem relatively normal," Rick said. "Why do you want to get involved in a crazy quest like this one? You're setting yourself up for ridicule."

Katy jerked her head to look at him. Had he just called her normal? She recalled no other instance in her entire life in which another person applied the term normal to her.

He'd asked a question. She really should answer it.

"First of all," she said, "it's not crazy. Second, I don't care what other people think of me. But to answer your question, I got involved because I want to understand these creatures we call Bigfoot. And if we can prove Bigfoot is real, that's icing on the cake."

"Hairy, smelly icing." She must've looked peeved again, because he held up a hand in surrender. "It was a dumb joke. I guess I don't understand how you can put up with the ridicule. But I admire your tenacity."

"Really."

He glanced out at the night, then back at her. "Have you ever seen a Bigfoot?"

A whooping cry echoed from the woods.

They both whipped their heads toward the sound. Rick sprang upright. Goosebumps erupted up and down Katy's arms. The cry had sounded even closer than the one she heard seconds before Rick stepped out onto the deck.

"What was it?" Rick asked, his voice sharp with tension. "An owl?"

He sounded as unconvinced as she was by his suggestion.

Deeper into the woods, matching cries answered the first, overlapping each other and then fading into nothing.

Katy whispered, "Those are no owls."

Rick stood frozen beside her, stiff and alert. Holding her breath, gaze locked on the woods, Katy listened for more cries. None came.

"I'll get a flashlight," Rick said.

He scurried back into the house, leaving the sliding doors open.

A scrabbling sound issued from below, closer than the woods. Something splashed in the creek.

Katy spun and bounded down the steps toward the rocky shore of the creek. Her shoes slipped on the wet rocks. She flailed her arms out for balance. Regaining her footing, she halted and listened.

Water gurgled. A faint breeze rattled the leaves in the trees.

The hairs on the back of her neck stiffened. Something was there, just across the creek from her. She sensed its presence like a wave of static electricity coursing over her. Holding perfectly still, she strained to see a shape on the other shore.

"Uh-uh."

The grunting issued from across the creek.

Her heart hammered. She tried to think of what to do, but her thoughts came in jumbled, colliding spurts.

A series of grunts, soft as whispers, emanated from the unseen visitor.

Footsteps clomped on the deck. Rick shouted, "Katy?"

On the opposite shore, water splashed.

An inhuman shriek split the night air. Footfalls raced away from the creek toward the woods.

Rick turned on a hand-held spotlight. The wide, blinding beam landed square on Katy. She threw up a hand to shield her eyes.

"There," she hollered, pointing across the creek.

Rick swung the beam in that direction. Katy glimpsed a dark shape ducking into the woods. A bipedal shape.

She took off after it.

Rick's footfalls pounded down the steps.

Her foot slipped. Momentum thrust her forward. She flung out her arms, but could not stop her fall. Her knees sank into the water, hitting bottom. She flopped face-first into the creek. The breath exploded from her an instant before her face slammed into the mud.

A pair of strong hands grasped her around the waist, hauling her out of the water.

Rick deposited her on her feet in front of him. Water poured off of her. She brushed her soaking hair away from her face and looked up at Rick.

"Thanks for the helping hand," she said.

"No problem. Band geeks have to stick together." He frowned at her. "What were you thinking? If that had been a bear—"

"Trust me, it was no bear." She thought back to her glimpse of the visitor. Though at the time she felt certain the creature was bipedal, she had no concrete evidence on which to base her assessment. "I'm not sure what it was, but I seriously doubt it was a bear. The black bears we have around here aren't that big."

He ran his gaze up and down her body. "Are you hurt?"

She shook her head.

The beam from the spotlight shined on them from the spot ten feet away where Rick had set the light on the ground. He marched to the spotlight, snatched it up, and aimed it at the woods.

"Whatever it was," he said, "it's gone now."

A silhouette appeared on the deck. Charlie called, "Everything okay?"

"Yeah," Rick said. "Katy got a little overexcited about a bear."

She started to hiss a retort, when she noticed his playful smirk. Strange, she thought. First he harangued her about believing in Bigfoot, and now he joked about it as if they were friends.

Men were weird.

Katy took hold of her shirt's hem and wrung it to release the water. A stream dribbled onto the ground. The night was cool, and she was beginning to feel a chill.

"We better get you inside," Rick said.

He ushered her back up the steps and into the house, sliding the door shut behind them. Charlie had already returned to the great indoors, where he was busy washing the dishes.

"I should go home," Katy said. "Get out of these wet clothes. I think I've had enough excitement for one evening."

Rick nodded.

To Charlie, Katy said, "I'll talk to you tomorrow."

"Sure thing."

Rick took hold of Katy's elbow. "I'll walk you out."

Charlie smiled and winked at Katy. She shook her head. Sneaky old coot.

A few minutes later Katy and Rick stood beside her car in the driveway. She opened the driver's door, pausing to look at him. He said nothing.

"Bye," she said.

He nodded.

Sighing, she climbed into the car and shut the door. Rick stood alongside the car, hands in his jeans pockets. She started the engine.

Rick rapped on the window.

She rolled it down and peered up at him. "Yes?"

Leaning closer, he said, "I acted like a jerk earlier tonight. I'm sorry."

"Okay."

He met her gaze. "Does this mean we're friends?"

She smiled. "Of course. Band geeks have to stick together, right?"

He returned the smile. "Right."

She rolled up the window, buckled her seatbelt, and drove away. Maybe there was hope for Rick yet.

Take off on an adventure!

with the novels in

THE HUMAN ORIGINS SERIES

by

LISA A. SHIEL

BOOK 1

THE HUNT FOR BIGFOOT

Katy and Rick tumble into a double-edged mystery—a hidden Bigfoot society protected by an ancient race and a mysterious billionaire willing to kill to preserve the legend. Can they unravel an enigma half a billion years in the weaving?

BOOK 2

LORD OF THE DEAD

Continues Katy and Rick's quest for the truth about human origins and explores the debate between Egyptologists and New Age enthusiasts over the enigmatic Book of Thoth. This time, the fate of the human race itself is at stake.

BOOK 3

RELIC OF THE ANCIENT ONES

Around the world, someone is stealing seemingly unrelated ancient artifacts. Drawn into the mystery, Erin and Alex plummet headlong into shocking revelations about humanity's history, and its future, as they chase the evidence to the Grand Canyon and beyond.

BOOK 4

REVENGE OF THE ANCIENT ONES

Erin and Alex continue their quest for the relic. As they solve the mystery of its purpose and location, they uncover shocking facts about Erin's past and her connection to the relic.

**available from
your local bookstore, Amazon.com, BarnesAndNoble.com
or
www.JacobsvilleBooks.com**

About the Author

LISA A. SHIEL RESEARCHES AND WRITES ABOUT EVERYTHING strange, from Bigfoot and UFOs to alternative history and science. She has a master's degree in library science and previously served as president of the Upper Peninsula Publishers & Authors Association. As a fiction writer, Lisa blends her paranormal interests with sci-fi and romance elements to create her own brand of adventure stories. Her fiction works include short story collections as well as the other novels in the Human Origins Series—including *The Hunt for Bigfoot, Lord of the Dead*, and *Relic of the Ancient Ones*. Lisa's nonfiction books explore topics as diverse as Bigfoot, evolution, and Michigan's quirky history.

www.LisaShiel.com

www.ingramcontent.com/pod-product-compliance
Lightning Source LLC
Chambersburg PA
CBHW030631130626
46552CB00002B/789